LIL' SISTER

LIL' SISTER

ANA'GIA WRIGHT

www.urbanbooks.net

Urban Books
1199 Straight Path
West Babylon, NY 11704

ISBN- 13: 978-1-60162-039-2
ISBN- 10: 1-60162-039-X

First Printing June 2008
Printed in the United States of America

10 9 8 7 6 5 4 3 2 1

This is a work of fiction. Any references or similarities to actual events, real people, living, or dead, or to real locales are intended to give the novel a sense of reality. Any similarity in other names, characters, places, and incidents is entirely coincidental.

Submit Wholesale Orders to:
Kensington Publishing Corp.
C/O Penguin Group (USA) Inc.
Attention: Order Processing
405 Murray Hill Parkway
East Rutherford, NJ 07073-2316
Phone: 1-800-526-0275
Fax: 1-800-227-9604

Acknowledgments

I must give thanks to the deities who have blessed me with this gift and for giving me the strength and courage to share it with others. Special thanks to my parents for providing me with the foundation to explore the unknown and instilling in me the desire to achieve great things.

My agent, Missy Brown, for her tolerance of me during this literary journey and for believing in me. A very special thank you to Lawanda D. and Lisa F. for all of your hours of poring over my words only to send me back pages and pages of red ink. I still love y'all for it.

Thanks to every member of the Indigo Ink writers' group for your honesty, criticism and encouragement. Special thanks to Jana Jay for give me the opportunity to be a member of your group and making available a venue to perfect the craft.

Prologue

Krystal finished the instant message she was writing to her sister. Glancing over the short message, satisfied of its discreet content, she pressed the send button. Tonight, well, tonight she'd leave all of the pain behind. She stood over her duffel bag, checking everything twice, making sure she didn't leave anything behind. Once she was out of this place, it'd be a cold day in hell before she returned.

You're only thirteen years old. You don't have a job and you don't have anywhere to go. If you're going to live in my house, you're going to live by my rules.

Her father's words echoed through her mind. She'd show him. They thought she didn't have any place to go, but she knew otherwise. They'd miss her when she was gone.

She grabbed two more purses from her closet and her favorite pair of Nike tennis shoes and shoved them into the bag. Zipping it closed, she slung its weight over her shoulder. Snatching the power cord from the wall, she silently packed her laptop and wireless Internet card into a separate bag. She grabbed her two-way pager from the nightstand and snapped its clip to the belt looped around her twenty-four-inch waist. The last items she picked up were a stuffed bear she adored and her framed picture of Jerad, her first love. She was all packed and ready to go.

She surveyed the room one last time. She'd miss her queen-sized waterbed. It always seemed to know how to slowly sway her to sleep. The butterscotch walls that had taken her and her father a week to paint to perfection stared back at her. She took one last glance at the stuffed animals collected over the few years of her life, scattered here and there with no real home of their own, and sighed. She had to leave it all behind for her sanity, she had convinced herself. She was tired of the fighting with her parents. They didn't understand her and they didn't seem to want to.

She thought back to the time when the fights first started. She remembered the scream that left her body when she'd found her first love dead. Though she never recalled walking over to him, cradling his limp body in her arms, the stillness of his body stayed with her.

Krystal blinked back fresh tears. She missed him so much. Her parents just didn't understand. He meant the world to her. He truly understood her. Jerad had never done anything to disrespect her. He treated her like a lady and he never pressured her into doing anything. Her parents were convinced he was molesting her, but truth be told, he never once tried to touch her in that way. She tried to make them understand, but she just couldn't bring herself to say the words.

The neighbors found them, Jerad's dead body lying in her arms, both wrists slit. They took her next door and called his father. After the ambulance, police cars, and media had returned to their sanctuaries, Jerad's father came for her. All she could do was gaze up at him, tears streaming down her face.

"Why did he do it?" she'd managed.

He just stared back at her, just as grief-stricken as she.

They'd been through this a million times. They both knew sooner or later they'd be too late to save him. Krystal felt her heart sink. She had no right to mourn Jerad, not when his father stood before her. He'd lost the two most important people in his life. She still had her family. He didn't have anyone.

Krystal opened her arms to him. He sat down beside her and hugged her. They cried together. They mourned Jerad together. He knew what she had seen. The neighbors had told him how they had found them both in the tub, her cradling him, yelling that he had promised her not to do this.

She never did get the chance to say her final good-bye. Her parents forbade her from going to the funeral, saying it was for Jerad's family. They just didn't get it. Jerad was just as much her family as they were. His father waited for her outside of the school that following week. He gave her a program from the funeral and a note neatly folded in a sealed envelope. She never opened the note.

That's when the fights started. Every time she went somewhere, her parents wanted to know where she was going. She got tired of them questioning her every move, every phone call, every glance out the window, so she just locked them out of her life. She'd come home from school and head straight for her room. Most of the time, she wouldn't even come out for dinner. At first, they came up and asked if she was okay. She always heard them coming, giving her time enough to dry her face and turn open a book. She'd always say she was fine, just studying, but in reality she was an emotional wreck.

Can't let them think I'm a baby. Gotta get it together, girl, she told herself. And she did. For the next few months she pretended everything was copacetic when she was around people. Everything was fine until they found the program. Then again, all hell broke loose.

Well, this was it. She was done. That was the last argument she intended on having with them. It was nearly midnight. They probably wouldn't even miss her. She closed the bedroom door and slowly crept out of the house.

Their house stood on the corner of a dark, winding road with no sidewalks or speed limits. Many nights her family barely escaped being run down by some drunken teenager who'd misjudged the giant hill and sharp curve standing before her. Although they survived, most nights the lawn wasn't so lucky.

Krystal slowly started her ascent of the massive hill. She had a long road ahead of her, but she refused to submit to the little voice in her head telling her that she was making a huge mistake. Within minutes she reached the secret hideaway. It wasn't much, merely the back of the fruit stand at the junction of her street and the main road.

She slid between the two broken pickets in the fence. The roof of the building hung over the rear, providing shade from the summer sun, shelter from rain, and a quaint little retreat she and her sister shared exclusively. The hideaway was just far enough away to keep prying eyes from spying on them, but close enough that when they wanted to get away they could walk the distance. When her eyes finally focused from the glow of the flashlight, Krystal was surprised to see her older sister sitting on one of the stools they had hidden behind the building. She'd expected to beat her sister there but apparently, Myisha had other ideas.

"Krystal, why are you doing this?" Myisha asked as she watched her sister step through the opening in the fence.

"Don't try to talk me out of this. You have no idea what it's like living with them. It was bad enough living in your shadow. They never say the words, but the 'why can't you be more like your sister' is always there. I can't do this anymore. If I stay in that house another minute, I'm gonna end up just like Jerad."

"You don't mean that."

"You have no idea. Had it not been for Jerad, I probably would have ended it all a long time ago."

Krystal hated that her sister had to find out about things this way. Only Jerad had known about her previous suicide attempt. She believed it was part of the reason he'd lived as long as he did. He always kept a close eye on her emotional state, ensuring she didn't slip back into the depression that had caused her initial attempt.

Over the past three years he'd seen a significant change in her emotional well-being. As she matured, he'd witnessed how she'd handled the deaths of two of her friends as well as her uncle. He'd waited until he felt she was strong enough to deal with his death before he ended his life.

"So where are you going?"

"The Trio's coming to get me."

"That's not what I asked you." Myisha made a not so pleasant face at her younger sister.

"Look, The Trio has been there when no one else has. His cousins watched over Jerad as best they could. He was family to them and they see me the same way. I think it's best that I keep the rest to myself."

"Krystal, Mom and Dad are going to worry about you."

"You think I haven't thought about that?" Krystal stood and began pacing. She was losing her patience. "I don't have a choice right now. For my sanity, I have to do this. Wouldn't you rather me leave and live, or would you prefer I stay here and die?"

"Stop saying that. You're not going to kill yourself."

"And what makes you think that? You've been gone for five years. You talk to them more than you talk to me. When's the last time you asked me what was going on in my life?"

"That's not fair and you know it. I've been away at

school. I've had to go through adjustments just like you have."

"You know what, forget it. I shouldn't have told you, either."

Krystal heard what sounded like tires on the gravel parking lot on the other side of the fence. She turned to see the glow from the headlights of the SUV. By the time she gathered her bags and purse, they were honking the horn.

"Look. That's my ride. I gotta go."

"You sure you wanna do this?" Myisha asked as she hugged her sister. She still wished Krystal would reconsider.

"Myisha, I have to." Krystal pulled away from her and handed her a card with a number on it. "Here's my number. I'll call you once I get settled in."

"What am I supposed to tell Mom and Dad?"

"You'll think of something," she yelled back as she slid through the opening in the fence.

Krystal slowly walked over to the man standing by the rear door of the Lexus SUV. He opened the door for her and helped her inside. When he was sure she was comfortable, he closed the door and climbed into the front passenger seat. The driver put the truck in reverse, pulled out of the parking lot and into the street.

Krystal watched as her sister waved good-bye. Slowly Myisha became a speck in the night until she disappeared completely. As Krystal's old life faded in the distance, she felt numb. Things were as they should be. She'd convinced herself of that. Jerad had given her the opportunity to start fresh, and that's exactly what she planned on doing.

Chapter One

Four years had past since Krystal had found her first love's cold dead body lying in a pool of tepid water. It felt like only yesterday when she'd entered the apartment where her life had changed. Initially, her mind refused to comprehend the sight. She'd dreamt of him the night before; saw him floating behind her closed eyelids. She didn't want to believe the images, the buckled floors, splashes of watered-down red, but her dreams never lied.

She remembered hearing the scream leave her body, still felt the hot tears as they'd streamed down her face. She didn't remember walking over to him or cradling his limp body in her arms. She somehow managed to crawl into the tub and crossed his arms over his chest. He was so cold. He'd lost so much blood. So much water.

She'd stared at the familiar scenery on the way to school, not really seeing anything that her gaze rested upon. She'd hoped to be greeted by the sound of birds singing and the sun drying the tears from her eyes, but the rumble of thunder that shook the classroom walls and the darkened sky reminded her of the sadness this day held. Lightning, the visual manifestation of nature's fury, momentarily lit up the sky. But it was heaven's tears that Krystal related to so well. The water pelted the window, propelled by the velocity of the fierce wind.

Today was going to be a long day, and she wasn't looking forward to it.

"Miss Bao, is there something outside of that window more important than your education?" the nun standing in front of the white board asked.

Krystal rolled her eyes and sucked her teeth, not wanting to be bothered with the nuns or school today. She had enough on her mind. She wished Andre had allowed her to stay home. It was the anniversary of Jerad's death, for God's sake. Letting her stay home was the least he could have done.

"No, ma'am." Krystal faced the nun, ignoring the snickering from her classmates. "May I please be excused? I'm not feeling too well. I think I need to see the nurse."

The nun looked her over one good time. Her color did seem a bit off today, and she hadn't been paying attention since the beginning of class, which was unusual. The sister thought something might be wrong, but she didn't want to say anything.

"Go ahead. Make sure you bring back a note."

Krystal closed her notebook and gathered her things. Although all eyes should have returned to the front of the classroom, Krystal's classmates paid more attention to her gathering her belongings than to the nun proceeding with today's lesson.

She took her time gathering the remainder of her books and the numerous doodles of crosses and caskets she'd drawn this morning. Swinging her backpack over her shoulder, she grabbed her purse and made her way to the door. She hesitated only for a moment in front of her best friend's desk. China looked up at her and signaled she'd give her a call later. Then, assured she'd have someone to talk to who understood her plight, Krystal exited the classroom, heading for the nurse's office.

Each step required effort, her movements weighed with years of harbored grief and sorrow. Four years ago today her life had sunk into the depths of despair. Too young to know how to cope, too isolated for anyone else to understand, she somehow managed to make it day to day.

Krystal fought back the tears as she approached the nurse's office. She tried her best to pull things together. She just needed to be strong for a little while longer. She just needed to keep it together long enough to convince the nurse she wasn't well enough to stay at school.

She opened the door, stepping into the well-lit white office. God, she hated the nurse's office. Though it was bright, it always felt cold and sterile. Though her eyes remained fixed on the floor, she caught a glimpse of the school nurse sitting behind her maple wood desk, leaning back in her chair.

"I see you made it through half of the day this time. I expected to see you in my office earlier." She leaned forward, crossing her arms over the mound of paperwork perfectly centered on the desk.

"Only because I sit in the back of most of my classes and no one pays me any attention," Krystal replied as she dropped her book bag to the floor.

"Have a seat." She gestured toward one of the two chairs on the other side of the desk, watching as the obviously upset teenager trudged her way across the office.

"Thanks."

Krystal lost the battle with the tears long before she gained any comfort from the twill chair. Lowering her eyes, burying her face in her hands, she quietly wept. She hated feeling this way. She wanted to accept that he was gone. Deep down, though, something refused to allow her to be at peace with it.

Glancing up, Krystal watched through tear-filled eyes as the woman behind the desk picked up the phone. Expecting the woman to ask her for a phone number, Krystal prepared to say the numbers, only to see the nurse dial a five-digit number she couldn't quite make out.

Yohan fidgeted in his seat in a corner of the office at Krystal's school. He'd been there since early this morning, under the constant scrutiny of some teenaged girl working in the office. Andre had told him that Krystal was unusually quiet on the drive to school this morning. He knew why. The significance of today had a great deal to do with it. He still couldn't believe the Trio had insisted she attend school today of all days. Yet here he was sitting in the office, waiting for the call that Krystal needed to go home.

Today was Krystal's day of mourning. For the last four years, he stood by her side not only as her man, but as her friend, supporting her on this day. Jerad's name was never mentioned in their home except on this day. For hours she'd talk about him, recounting hour by hour the last few days they shared. But she always stopped in the same place. He never once heard her speak of the day Jerad died.

None of them, not even the members of The Trio, knew of the events of that day. None of them dared ask, either. They respected Krystal's privacy, so they allowed her to hold on to her memories of Jerad in any manner she saw fit. No one spoke of that day to her, and outside of her few attempts to attend school on this day, she only allowed Yohan to spend time with her on her day of mourning.

A hush surrounded him in the office most of the morning. He found himself drifting off to sleep within an hour of his arrival. He didn't know whether to be relieved or angry when the vibration from his pager snatched him from a troublesome dream. Reading the message, his lips turned down in disgust. He quickly entered a reply, pressed the send button, and proceeded to turn the two-way off.

Yohan stretched and shifted in his seat, trying to once again get comfortable but having very little luck. As he stood, prepared to take a walk to get some blood circulating in his legs, one of the office phones rang. Turning to walk out of the door, the young lady at the desk furthest away called his name. He'd told them to let him know if Krystal needed someone to take her home. He'd picked her up on a number of occasions; everyone in the office knew him, so no one questioned his being there.

The young lady motioned him toward her desk. "Mr. Hampton?"

Making his way over to where she sat, Yohan observed the concern on the young woman's face. In that moment, he wondered what had been said on the phone.

"Krystal is in the nurse's office. When you go out the door, make a right and it's the third door on the left."

He thanked her, then turned and exited the office. As he made his way down the hall, he passed two teenaged girls skipping class. They smiled and waved as he approached. He thought about reprimanding them, but decided instead to ignore their pitiful attempt at attention. He heard one of them make a comment as he continued down the hall, but he ignored that as well.

Knocking lightly on the door, Yohan waited for a reply from inside. When he heard the woman say "come in," he opened the door and stepped into the small office. Krystal sat in a ball in one of the chairs, rocking and weeping. She always rocked when she was upset. When she'd first started sleeping in his bed, it drove him nearly crazy. Now he rarely noticed it.

Yohan squatted in front of her, securing her hands in his.

"I'll give you two a moment." The nurse stood. She glanced down at Krystal one last time before heading for the door.

"Can you get her some water?"

"Sure." She stepped from the room, giving the young couple some time alone.

"Wanna talk about it?"

"Why'd they make me come? They knew I couldn't handle this." Her head shook, the tears racing down her cheeks as she tried to hold on to what little control she still possessed. "I wanna go home."

"Shh, I know, baby." Yohan pulled the weeping girl into his embrace. He could feel her body trembling with each gasp. He needed to calm her down before she started to hyperventilate. Holding on to her, rocking her in his arms, doing what little he could to make everything better, Yohan prayed for the strength to help her through this.

In his mind, though, he just didn't understand why she was even here. The Trio knew how hard this day was for her, and yet they'd forced her to go to school anyway. This had to end. He refused to allow them to do this to her again. From now on, if she didn't feel up to coming to school on this day, he wasn't going to let anyone make her.

A soft knock drew his attention and within seconds, the nurse stepped through the door. She handed Yohan a bottle of water for Krystal.

"Here." He twisted the top off and handed her the bottle. "Drink this, and then I'll take you home."

"Mr. Hampton, may I speak with you, please?" The woman didn't wait for a reply. She just stepped through the door confident he'd be two steps behind her.

Looking down at Krystal, wiping away a stray tear with his thumb, he helped her back into the seat. "Finish your water. I'll be back in a minute." He kissed her on the forehead and exited the office, pulling the door securely shut behind him.

"She needs help," the woman said, pushing her glasses up from the tip of her nose.

"I know. We've tried everything: psychologist, psychiatrist, counselors, groups. She just won't open up. She's usually okay. It's just this day."

Last year China had provided the nurse with a little information regarding Krystal's mood on this day, but the girl refused to tell her the full story. It was her job to find out if there was something going on, possibly in Krystal's home, which had her in tears each year on this day.

"I've never asked her, but what happened on this day?"

"Four years ago,"—he lowered his eyes, not able to look her in the face when he said the words—"her first love killed himself." Yohan didn't know why it was hard for him to tell her. It wasn't like he'd ever met Jerad, and yet the fact that Krystal was in so much pain did something to him.

"My God. How?" Stunned, the woman didn't know what else to say. Krystal was so young and she couldn't begin to imagine what that teenaged girl had been through.

"His father said he found him in the tub with his wrists slit. Every year on this day she gets like this. She'll be back to herself tomorrow." He glanced at the door, feeling the need to reach out to Krystal but having no idea how.

"Just keep a close watch on her. She's in a very fragile state. I wouldn't advise leaving her alone."

"I'll take good care of her. She just needs to mourn." Yohan turned from the woman and reentered the room. He lifted Krystal's backpack and purse from the floor and wrapped his arm around her shoulder. "Come on. Let's get you home."

As they walked, he was glad the hallway was empty. Apparently the two girls skipping class had found a new corridor to occupy. The two lone figures walked in silence through the two steel doors at the end of the hall and out into the overcast day.

Stopping in mid-stride, Yohan pulled Krystal into a loving embrace.

"Thanks for coming to get me. You're too good to me sometimes."

"Shh . . . its fine. That's what real men do for their women. You should know that by now."

As they stood in the hallway, Yohan's attention turned in the direction of a red truck pulling up behind his vehicle at the other end of the parking lot. He watched as it stopped. He expected someone to get out, but they didn't. The tint of the windows obstructed his view, and as the truck drove away, he felt foolish. It was probably just someone looking for something and they just happened to stop behind him.

He scooped Krystal into his arms, feeling the need to have her close to his heart. He hated to see her hurting, but the only thing he could do was be there for her when she was ready to deal with this. He carried her across the parking lot, secured her in the passenger seat of his truck. He'd take her to the one place he knew she needed to go. Home.

Chapter Two

Aubrey Fedichi pulled into a parking space in front of Krystal's school fuming, still not believing his brother sent her to school today. They'd been through this a million times. There was one day Krystal was guaranteed to miss school, and today was the day. As far as he was concerned, there was no excuse for Andre sending her to school.

He made his way through the double doors, passing a number of students and teachers as he stormed toward the office. Many of the nuns spoke as he passed. They knew him and his brothers. They'd all attended the private school when they were younger.

He swung open the door to the office; a number of concerned faces immediately turning in his direction.

The stout woman with glasses at the front desk leaned over, trying to get a closer look at the familiar face. "Aubrey. We haven't seen you in ages. What brings you here?"

His frown turned to a slight smile the moment he recognized the woman who'd been the school secretary for nearly thirty years. "I came to get my sister, Krystal Bao. Do you know where her next class is?"

"I'm sorry, Aubrey. Ms. Bao left around noon with Mr. Hampton." She took in the healthy physique of the eldest Fedichi. She'd found them all quite handsome, the spitting image of their father.

"At least someone has some damn sense," he said under his breath.

"I'm sorry. Did you say something?"

"No. Thanks anyway." He turned and made his way back to his car. Sliding into the driver's seat, he picked up his cell phone and dialed Yohan's number. His fingers drummed the steering wheel as he waited for an answer.

" 'Sup Brey?"

"Krystal with you?" *Okay, that was a stupid question. Of course Krystal is with him.*

"Yeah. She's in the tub." Yohan grabbed a can of soup from the pantry and pulled the tab to open it.

"Thanks, man. I owe you."

"No biggie. She is my responsibility after all. Why'd Dre make her go to school anyway?" Leaning against the counter, he poured the contents of the can into a pot.

"You know how he is when he gets in his moods. He got into it with ole girl last night. He probably just didn't want to be bothered."

"That ain't no excuse. He knew she wouldn't be there long. I told him I was coming right back to get her. It wasn't like he was really going to have to watch her."

"Why'd you drop her at Dre's anyway?" Normally, Aubrey stayed out of Yohan's business, but this affected all of them and he wanted an answer.

"I had a run I needed to make earlier and I couldn't have her with me. Needless to say, I was hella mad when I got back and he told me he took her to school. I was at the school within twenty minutes. I figured one of her teachers would send her to the office when she was ready to go. We just got home about an hour ago."

"How is she?" Aubrey was really worried about Krystal. Each year they'd watched as she sunk further and further into her depression.

"I've never seen her this bad. She hasn't said a word since we left her school."

Aubrey lowered his head. He hated to see her torturing herself this way, but a feasible solution as to how to help her eluded him. They went through this every year with her. She'd sink into herself, refusing to talk or eat or do anything other than wallow in her sorrow.

"Has she eaten?" Aubrey asked.

"Not yet. I'm making her some soup."

"Well, see if you can get her to eat. I'll be over there a little later tonight to check on her."

"I'll try. Hey, can you make sure China gets a ride home? I was supposed to come get her after cheerleading practice, but Krystal's in no condition to be left alone and I don't think she'll be up to leaving the house."

"Yeah. I'll make the arrangements. I'm still at the school. I'll leave a message for her at the office. You just worry about making sure Krystal has everything she needs."

"You know she's in good hands."

Aubrey made the arrangements for China and hopped on the interstate to tend to some business before going to check on Krystal. They were all worried. Tonight, though, was going to be a long night for everyone.

Krystal climbed from the cool bathwater and used the extra large fluffy towel to dry off. She didn't feel like getting dressed, so she grabbed the silk bathrobe from the hook on the back of the door and slipped it on. She inhaled the soothing aroma of lavender and vanilla filling the air in the spacious bathroom. Staring into her blood-shot eyes in the mirror, she finally realized she could no longer keep her secret. In order to regain control over her life, she first needed to read Jerad's letter and then talk about that day.

Gathering her thoughts, she opened the bathroom door and trudged over to the chair where her purse lay. Staring at the bag, thoughts of Jerad flooded her mind. She fought back the tears as she opened the flap and pulled the sealed white envelope from the inside pocket. Twirling the envelope between her fingers, it seemed heavier this time, like the weight of the sorrow seeped from the seams. She somehow made her way to the bed, not remembering moving or sitting down.

Dumping the contents of the envelope on the down comforter, she allowed the articles to fall where they may. The first item she reached for was the program from Jerad's funeral. Her hand hovered over his image, remembering before she picked up the half-folded paper. Running her fingers over the picture, the memories of the day he died came floating back to her. She closed her eyes, allowing the tears to fall as the images played over and over in her mind. She tried to shake them away, but they continued to seep from her subconscious.

Krystal shuddered as she remembered how cold Jerad's body had felt in her arms. She'd tried to wake him, tried her best to get him to come back to her, to no avail. He was already gone, lost to her for all eternity.

No longer able to stare down into the perfectly round dark brown eyes of her first love, she allowed the paper to slip from her grasp. She grabbed the corner of the sealed letter he'd left for her from beneath a photograph. Although it was addressed to her, in the four years since his death, she'd never opened it. She'd come close many times, but she'd never truly been ready to know what was on the pages.

She gathered her courage and slipped her finger beneath the seal, ripping the envelope across the top. Inching the letter from the confines of the narrow white paper prison, she unfolded the sheets and stared at the neatly handwritten words on the page.

My dearest Krystal,

Baby, I am so sorry. I know I promised I wouldn't leave you, but I just can't do it anymore. I wish I was as strong as you. But I'm not. Mama came for me last night. She said it's time for me to come home. I've finished what I was sent here to do.

I've watched you grow into a beautiful young lady, and though I know my actions will hurt for a while, I want you to continue to grow. Continue to mature and become the strong black woman I know you are.

I'm going to be with Mama. My soul's going to be with her, but I'm leaving my heart with you. I told you we'd be together until death do us part. I'm just sorry it's so soon.

I'll always be with you, Krystal. Take some time to mourn then move on with your life. Go do all of those wonderful things we talked about. And most of all, keep yourself open to love.

With all my love, on my dying day,
Jerad

Krystal slid off of the bed, her weight dropping to the floor like a sack of potatoes. She wailed, allowing any pent-up emotion to pour from behind the wall she'd erected around her heart. She rocked as grief reared its ugly head. She yelled, beating her hands on the hardwood floor, asking again and again why he'd done this to her.

As Yohan removed the pot of soup from the stove, he heard Krystal's crying break the silence in the apartment. No sooner had he poured the contents of the pot into a bowl, her crying turned to screams. The soup being the least of his concerns, he rushed into the bedroom to find Krystal beating her fists into the floor. She kicked and screamed, no longer able to control her body as the anguish finally took over.

He grabbed her from behind, crossing her arms over her chest to keep her from hurting herself any further. She fought him with everything she had, trying her best to escape his grasp, but she wasn't strong enough. Krystal struggled in his arms for nearly twenty minutes before she began to relax. Her head hung low, her body weak with exhaustion. She turned her head ever so slightly to see him; then she closed her eyes and passed out.

Chapter Three

"I hope you're fuckin' happy," Aubrey spat at his brother Andre. He walked a narrow path, his head shaking from side to side in disbelief of what his brother had done.

"How the hell was I supposed to know this shit was going to happen?" He threw his hand up in the air, glaring at Brey, waiting for whatever answer might come.

"You know she wasn't supposed to go to school today and you sent her anyway."

"Stop it! The both of you just fuckin' stop it! Krystal doesn't need this right now." Antonio, the third member of The Trio, yelled at his two brothers. Them two going at each other wasn't going to make this any easier, and their attention needed to remain on helping Krystal.

"If his punk ass hadn't sent her to school this wouldn't have happened," Aubrey said under his breath.

"I don't think this had anything to do with her going to school," interjected the calm voice from the man standing at the window.

They all turned to face Yohan. He hadn't spoken a

word to any of them since they'd arrived. He'd been staring out of the window, absorbed in his own thoughts. Before he got the opportunity to explain his theory, the bedroom door opened and the doctor stepped through.

"How is she?" Yohan asked their neighbor. There was one thing Lincoln Heights had plenty of, and doctors was it.

"She's sleeping. I cleaned the cuts on her hands." He handed Yohan a tube of antiseptic cream. "Make sure she keeps this on them."

"What caused her to flip out like that?" Andre asked.

Antonio cut his eyes at his twin. He was just trying to make himself feel better. He was sure his brother was hoping the doctor was going to tell them this had nothing to do with her going to school.

"I wouldn't exactly call her behavior flipping out." He gave Andre a disapproving look. "From what Yohan has told me, she's showing classic symptoms of post-traumatic stress disorder. Has anything happened in her life lately that may have upset her?"

"You don't know the half of it. We'll get her the help she needs. Thanks for coming on such short notice." Yohan escorted the man to the door. He didn't want to go into detail about the letter. He knew what had triggered Krystal's episode. He just hoped now she'd realize she needed help.

The doctor looked at Yohan one last time before deciding to drop it. He'd lived in Lincoln Heights long enough to know The Trio took care of their own. When Krystal was ready to face whatever demons were troubling her, they'd make sure she got the best help money could buy.

"Don't look at me like that," Yohan said, turning his eyes from the scrutiny of the man standing in front of him.

"You know what triggered it, don't you?"

Releasing a sigh, he replied, "Yeah, I just hope now she's ready to deal with all of this."

"Look, I'm not a psychologist by any means, but if she continues like this—"

"Don't say it. I already know."

The doctor pulled a card from his pocket. "When Krystal's ready, call this number. She's a friend of mine and she's the best in her field. I think talking with her will do a world of good."

"I'll keep that in mind."

Stepping through the doorway, the doctor turned to make his way down the hall. Yohan slid the business card into his pocket as he watched the man descend the stairs.

"All right, Yohan, spill it," Andre said. They didn't keep secrets, and especially not about Krystal.

Andre, Aubrey, and Antonio—The Trio—sat in Yohan's living room gawking at him, arms crossed, feet tapping, fingers drumming and all. Ignoring their scrutiny, he dropped the letter on the table and walked into the bedroom to check on Krystal.

Yohan sat on the edge of the bed watching her sleep. He thought about the last time she'd talked about Jerad. She seemed in so much pain. She talked about the time he'd tried to shoot himself in the head. She'd walked in just as he was pulling the trigger. Seeing the tears in her eyes, knowing the pain he was about to cause her, Jerad chose to lower the weapon. Krystal pried the cold steel from his hand and they'd spent the night just holding each other.

Now, watching her sleep, knowing the agony she faced, he understood how she must have felt all of those years. For three years she'd been in his position, watching Jerad go through the same hurting she now harbored. They'd supported each other, ensuring that they each had what they needed to live through another day.

Up until now, Yohan hadn't understood why Jerad's suicide letter remained unopened. Each year since his death, they'd talked about him, and each year, she pulled the letter out. However, in all of those years, she'd never been able to bring herself to open it. Seeing her like this, though, knowing now what the letter contained, he understood her hesitance. She had to be in the right frame of mind. She needed to be ready for closure, and up until now, she hadn't been.

Yohan stood and made his way to the window. He stared out into the cold night sky. The moon had even retreated from the sorrow of this night, allowing total darkness to reign supreme. There had to be a way to get through to her, make her understand how much she was hurting herself by not facing her pain. The question now was how.

"He hadn't been dead long when I found him. . . ." Krystal's voice trailed off as she allowed Yohan time to comprehend what she'd just said.

He hadn't meant to wake her. She needed her rest. He'd only come into the room to avoid discussing the letter with The Trio and to be close to her if she needed him.

"His body was warm for a while then it slowly turned cold just like the water. Maybe he never was warm. Maybe my mind just wanted him to be, but the longer I lay in that tub, the colder he got."

Yohan didn't turn around as she spoke. He couldn't bear to see the pain in her eyes. "You were the one who found him?"

Her lack of a response was confirmation enough. He finally turned to face her. She'd pulled her knees up to her chest and buried her face in them. He wanted so much to reach out to her, but he was afraid. He didn't know how she'd react to him touching her. She seemed to want to talk, and he hoped she'd be willing to get some professional help dealing with this.

His heart sank as she looked up at him with tears streaming down her cheeks. "Does anyone else know?"

"No." Her eyes asked for some sort of escape. "I didn't know how to tell them," she pleaded, the anguish pouring out of her. "His neighbors found us in the tub. His father knows, but that's it."

"Oh, Krystal, I am so sorry." Yohan needed her in his arms. He needed to feel useful.

No longer comfortable with the short distance between them, he went to her, pulled her into his arms and allowed her to cry until she had nothing left to give. Then, he tucked her into bed and left her to get some much-needed rest.

Aubrey picked up the half-folded piece of paper from the coffee table. He released a heavy sigh as he read the words. Seeing all he needed to see, he passed the letter to his brothers for them to read. Aubrey laid his head on the back of the chair and closed his eyes. Things made sense now. They knew about the letter; Yohan had mentioned it a number of times. He'd told them how Krystal held on to it but she'd never been able to bring herself to open it.

His heart ached knowing the pain that blossoming young woman felt, and even more so now that he knew what the letter contained. He stood and made his way to the spot Yohan vacated moments earlier. The sound of the front door slamming pierced the air. He didn't have to turn around to know who'd left. Andre and Jerad had been real close. Jerad was like a son to him. Dre had his own pain to deal with; no need to worry about a grown man. Krystal, on the other hand, posed more concern. She was still young, and though she'd lost some of her friends to car accidents and shootings, none of them meant as much to her as Jerad had.

"We promised Jerad we'd take care of her. We're not doing a very good job." Antonio finished reading the letter his cousin had left for Krystal. Letting her deal with this on her own was no longer an option. They'd let this go on long enough.

"What do you propose? We can't force her to talk." At thirty-seven, he was the eldest member of The Trio. He felt most responsible for Krystal's current situation. They should have gotten her some help when she first came to them.

"That's just it. Before, I don't think she was ready. Maybe she is now."

Aubrey turned to look at his younger brother. Though Antonio was the youngest of the three, born nearly eight minutes after his twin Andre and a year after Aubrey, he was always the analytical one. When everyone else was caught up in emotion, Antonio looked objectively at a situation and came up with a solution no one else would have dreamed of.

"What makes you say that?"

"Think about it." Antonio tilted his head back, locking his fingers behind his neck. He turned his eyes toward the ceiling before continuing. "In all of these years, she's held on to the letter but never opened it. Maybe this is her way of telling us she needs some help."

"I hope you're right." Aubrey closed his eyes and lowered his head as Krystal's sobs slipped from beneath the bedroom door. He started to go to her, but he knew there was nothing he could do. Yohan would take care of her, give her the love and reassurance she needed.

Chapter Four

Twenty minutes after retreating into the bedroom he shared with Krystal, Yohan again joined Aubrey and Antonio in the living room. Aubrey stopped mid-stride as the door closed. He glanced in Antonio's direction then back at Yohan before asking, "How is she?"

"She's finally back to sleep." Yohan sat in the spot Andre previously occupied. "Where'd Dre go?"

The remaining brothers exchanged glances, each silently asking the other who should answer. Though Yohan knew of Jerad, he only knew of the situation from Krystal's perspective. They remembered the night when Andre found himself caught in the middle of a shoot-out between some members of the LHC, as the Lincoln Heights Crew was known, and a group of boys from another neighborhood. He'd left his weapon in the car with Jerad just in case something happened. Somehow, through the flying bullets, Jerad managed to sneak out of the car and over to where Andre bunkered down. They managed to get out of the situation unscathed, and from that day forward, Andre was forever indebted to Jerad. That debt was the main reason Krystal was here instead of back in Louisiana with her family.

"He needed to get some air," Antonio finally replied, hoping to sound convincing.

"How much do you two know about the day Jerad died?" Yohan waited, carefully observing both Antonio's and Aubrey's expressions.

"About as much as you, I guess. Why?" Antonio responded.

Aubrey turned back to the window, losing himself in the night as he listened to their conversation, but he'd only interject if he had something of importance to share.

"Well, Krystal just dropped another tidbit of information pertaining to the situation."

"And what's that?"

"She was the one who found Jerad's body."

Aubrey jerked around, not sure he'd heard correctly. They both looked at Yohan with disbelief. "You're kidding, right? I thought his father was the one who found him."

Yohan straddled a chair, folding his arms across the back. His eyes met with Aubrey's as he responded, "So did everyone else. She never told anybody. She said his neighbors found them in the tub."

"Looks like she's stronger than we gave her credit for." *God.* Aubrey could beat himself for not seeing this sooner. How could they have been so blind? She'd been living with this for four years now, and they'd had no clue.

"Yeah, but I think she's ready to face this. That letter opened her eyes. She knows now Jerad didn't want her to live like this. His wish was for her to live life to its fullest, and right now she's not doing that. She still misses him, but I think she knows what she's been doing to herself isn't what he wanted for her."

"What do you suggest?" Aubrey leaned against the wall, hoping that someone had an idea because at the moment, he was at a loss.

"She needs to rest. She still hasn't eaten and she's been crying all day. I'll watch over her tonight and make sure she has everything she needs."

"You want one of us to stay?" Although Krystal was Yohan's responsibility, she needed all of her family to get through this. Staying the night to help was the least they could do. Krystal wasn't the only one suffering, and Aubrey saw that in Yohan's eyes.

"No. I can handle it. I'll talk to her in the morning; try to get a feel for where her head is at and what she wants to do."

"She can't keep holding this in."

"We all know that, and I think she finally sees it as well." Yohan grabbed the cordless phone from the table. "I'll call China and have her get Krystal's homework." He walked into the kitchen, leaving Antonio and Aubrey in the living room to ponder the situation further.

"I still can't believe she's kept this secret this long," Antonio said, glancing at the door and then at his brother.

"Why not? Since the night we went and got her, she hasn't said so much as one word to us about Jerad."

"Still, it's been four years, man. That's a long time." Leaning forward, Antonio grabbed the letter. He read the words again, trying to put himself in Krystal's shoes.

"I just hope she hasn't been blaming herself."

"Me too, man. Me too. You want me to go after Dre? She's going to need all of us if she's going to get through this."

"Give him some time. He'll come around." Aubrey turned back to the window before he finished his thought. "At least I hope so."

* * *

Andre parked his El Camino in front of a beige house at the end of the block. Staring at the little red numbers on the car stereo, he realized it was nearly two in the morning. He'd tried drinking, smoking, and driving his troubles away to no avail.

Since reading Jerad's suicide letter, his mind had been totally screwed up. He needed a distraction, and though it might take a little persuasion, he'd get one here. He had enough alcohol and weed in his system to keep him hard all night, and he'd fuck all night if ole girl was up to it.

Sliding his key in the door, he stepped into darkness. He plopped down on the couch, taking a few minutes to get his head together. They'd had a big fight yesterday, ending with her storming out of his apartment. He hadn't heard from her all day. Still, he needed her right now and he hoped she'd understand that.

The whooshing of her of her flip-flops coming down the stairs drew his attention. He was able to just barely make out her silhouette at the bottom of the staircase.

"Why you sitting down here in the dark?" she said with an attitude.

She'd heard that loud-ass truck of his before he turned the corner, knowing he was headed in her direction. How dare he just show up at her doorstep at this hour, especially since they'd had a big fight the day before? The least he could have done was pick up the phone and call. Flipping the light on, she immediately knew something wasn't right.

He looked over at her, his eyes half closed and red. She'd only put on a sheer robe before coming down the stairs. He looked her up and down, wanting to run his hands over her nearly nude chocolate body. He didn't say a word to her; he just closed his eyes and laid his head back on the couch.

"Dre, baby, what's wrong?" She took a seat next to him, the smell of marijuana nearly burning her nose. He'd been smoking; not a good sign. Dre only resorted to smoking weed when he was at his wit's end. She knew something major must be bothering him.

When he didn't respond, she understood. He wasn't ready to talk about it. He'd come to her because she could give him the one thing he needed: a distraction. She didn't mind. He was her man, and regardless of what had gone on between them yesterday, he needed her.

She straddled him, wrapping her hands around his head and drawing him closer. While running her fingers through his hair, she kissed him. He responded to her unspoken request, darting his tongue in and out of her mouth. Grabbing a handful of hair, he pulled her head back, trailing kisses down her neck. She unbuckled his belt and unbuttoned his pants. Pulling him from the confines of the cloth, she slid him into her, wanting sex.

She'd give him what he needed. If it took all night, she'd ease his mind for just a little while. She'd work him into exhaustion and then let him sleep. They had plenty of time to talk, but right now he needed one thing and one thing only—her.

Chapter Five

Krystal woke to the sound of birds singing and sunshine beaming through the window. Opening her eyes to the light, she rolled over expecting Yohan to be sound asleep in the bed next to her. Instead, she found him stretched out in a chair, eyes wide, staring at her.

"Good morning," she said, rolling over onto her side to get a better look at her man. He looked up at her with swollen eyes, and she was more than sure he hadn't slept a wink.

"Is it really?" What to say to her? He fought the urge to crawl into the bed and pull her into his arms. They needed to talk, but she had to be ready.

"Yeah. It is." She leaned up and the room spun. She lay back down to stop the throbbing behind her eyes.

Seeing the distress on her face, Yohan went to her. "Are you all right?" he asked, sitting down on the edge of the bed next to her.

"Just dizzy."

"You didn't eat yesterday. Lay back down. I'll get you some juice."

Krystal sunk back into the comfort of the pillow-top

mattress and goose-down pillows. Her stomach twisted in knots, a reminder of her neglect the day before.

Yohan returned with a glass of apple juice and a bowl of instant grits. Since coming to Atlanta, Krystal had fallen in love with grits. She'd grown up eating cream of wheat, but now preferred the texture of her recently discovered favorite food.

Yohan watched her swirl the butter around the bowl before placing a spoonful in her mouth. Within minutes, the bowl and glass were empty. As he took the dishes from her, he noticed she seemed more relaxed.

"Better?" he asked.

"Much. Thanks. You take care of me so well."

"I just wish you'd take better care of yourself." He allowed her to think about what he'd just said while he took the dishes into the kitchen.

Krystal gazed out into the beautiful morning sky. Her friends should all be at school by now. She was glad he'd let her go to sleep. She wasn't in the mood to deal with school today.

"Let me see your hands," Yohan said as he reentered the room and stood by the bed.

She held them out for him to see. He pulled the tube of antiseptic cream from the drawer in the nightstand and rubbed a bit of it into her now healing wounds.

"What happened to my hands?" She watched him tend to the task, wondering how her hands had gotten so beat-up.

"You don't remember?"

Looking up at him, her eyes wide and her eyebrows pulled together, she replied, "No."

"Don't worry about it. We'll talk about it later. So what do you feel like doing today?" He recapped the cream and slid the tube back into the drawer.

"Can we go to the park?"

"I know the perfect place. Go get dressed. I'll pack us a lunch and we can go whenever you're ready."

An hour later, Yohan pulled to a stop at the entryway to High Falls. He and Krystal came to the falls every spring since she'd moved in with The Trio. They'd always go just as the flowers began to bloom. They were long overdue for this year's trip, so he thought it the perfect opportunity to come.

"I didn't know you were bringing us out here." Krystal's lips turned up in a smile. Her eyes scanned the lake as they pulled into a parking spot.

"I know. Come on, the falls are waiting." He helped her out of the vehicle. She paused, her eyes locking with that of a man creeping past them in a red SUV. She didn't know why, but the intensity of his gaze sent a cold shudder up her spine.

Yohan's arms tightened around her, pulling her attention away from the back of the passing vehicle. "You ready to go?"

She smiled up at him. "Yeah, I'm ready to go."

The couple walked hand in hand down the first set of stairs leading to the falls. They stopped as they approached an area leveled off for visitors to watch the water make its initial descent over the rocks. He inched his arms around her waist as they stared off into the mist forming above the rushing water.

"I miss him so much sometimes." Krystal wanted to talk about Jerad. She wanted to get this out of her system once and for all. That letter opened her eyes and now, she was ready to face whatever life threw at her.

"I know you do. But Krystal, you can't keep doing this. This isn't what he wanted for you."

"I know that now and I'm ready to do something about it. I can't do this alone anymore. As much as I un-

derstand how he felt, I don't want to end up like him."
She wrapped her fingers around his thumb, brushing
against his knuckles. She took comfort being in his arms
and for a moment, life felt a little easier.

"I won't let anything happen to you. As long as you
need me, I'm here. We're all here for you." He rested his
chin on the top of her head as he stared out into the mist.
He wanted so much for her, but right now she needed to
make some serious decisions about her life.

"So now what?" The moment of truth, the pivotal
point in her life opened for her taking.

"Now, you relax and enjoy yourself."

For the next few hours, she put Jerad and all of her
worries out of her mind. Yohan babied her, making sure
she had anything she wanted. They spent most of the
time talking about how things were for her when she'd first
come to Lincoln Heights. She wanted things to be that
way again. She wanted to smile and laugh and enjoy life.

She missed her sleepovers with China and the weekend trips to Savannah and Hilton Head they used to
take. She'd never said anything to him about it since
their escapades had dwindled off, but now that she had
time to relive what she was missing, she wanted to make
a conscious effort to get those things back.

"I had no idea you felt this way. You should have told
me." Yohan wrapped his arms around her as they
watched a pair of ducks swim across the lake that fed the
falls. He'd gotten caught up in being The Trio's partner in
crime, and he'd been neglecting her. Showing no indication of unhappiness, he'd assumed everything between
them was fine.

Krystal rolled over so she could look Yohan in the face.
From the corner of her eye, she caught a glimpse of those
same dark eyes staring at her across the open field on
their side of the lake. The man must have realized she

was watching him because he turned and headed toward the playground.

"I didn't think it bothered me until now. I look back at how things were and what we used to have, and then I see where we are now, and I just don't feel the same. I know we've both grown, and maybe that's the problem. We've grown comfortable with how things are now. The things that once excited us got pushed in the background when we started living day to day."

"We can get the spark back. I'm willing to try if you are." He brushed the tip of her nose with his finger, sending a rush of loving desire from him to her.

"You know I am. I love you and I don't want to lose you."

Yohan's heart softened at Krystal's confession. In the last two years, he'd become more than just her bodyguard; he'd become her friend and more recently her lover. They hadn't told The Trio about their relationship for fear of the outcome. Though they considered him to be one of their own, neither he nor Krystal was sure how the guys would react to knowing that they were more than they appeared to be.

Now, though, hearing her say the words for the first time, Yohan thought it best they told The Trio. He'd wait a little while—at least until Krystal had begun therapy for her issues with Jerad's death—but they needed to tell The Trio soon. He loved her too, and he was tired of hiding his feelings.

Yohan leaned down and kissed her like he'd never kissed her before. A sudden rush of wanting swept them under, causing him to release a guttural moan through her body. He pulled away, the need to have her becoming overwhelming. Ending the kiss, he drew her into a loving embrace.

"I love you too, baby. I love you too."

After spending another hour surrounded by the calm of nature, the couple gathered their belongings and headed home. As they pulled on to the highway, Yohan made a call to The Trio. As a whole, the group decided to meet at Andre's apartment.

Everyone planned to be there: Aubrey and his wife, Andre and his girl, along with Antonio. The guys thought Krystal might need some female support, and the ladies were more than willing to help. They'd all become a close-knit family, and if one of them needed support, the others were there for the long haul.

Yohan turned to Krystal as he put the vehicle in park. She'd been awfully quiet during the ride home. More than sure that she had plenty on her mind, he'd decided to let her gather her thoughts before they went into this family meeting. He watched her stare blankly out of the window, deep in contemplation of her situation.

"Krystal?" She turned to face him, fear in her eyes. "It's going to be okay. We're only here to help you. You just have to let us."

"I'm scared, Yohan. What if I can't get through this?" Her eyes glazed over as the fear snatched hold of any hope remaining within her.

"It's not about you getting through this. We're in this together. You're not alone. We'll get through this." He intertwined his fingers with hers. "If you're not ready for this, I can call it off."

She hesitated, her gaze drifting up to the window of Andre's apartment. They were up there waiting. Waiting for her. Waiting to help her. She sunk into herself, mustering up enough courage to face what she so needed to face.

"Don't do that."

Fresh hot tears burned streaks down each of her cheeks. He hated seeing her like this. She should be smiling, happy. Instead, here she sat, facing the second toughest decision of her short life. Krystal's happiness would only come if she opened up and faced what she'd discovered the night Jerad died. She was strong, Jerad made sure of that, but she needed to realize they were there to help her.

"Come on. What's with the tears? Think of this as a new beginning."

For the first time since they'd headed home, Krystal smiled up at him. He was right. Pulling herself together, she made the decision to face her past. The sooner she faced it, the brighter her future would be.

"Okay," she said, taking in a deep breath then releasing it with a huff. "I'm ready."

All eyes turned in their direction as Yohan and Krystal entered the apartment. This was technically Krystal's real home. When The Trio first picked her up, she moved in with Andre. She had her own bedroom and bathroom and for the most part, free reign to do as she pleased. The only stipulations of her remaining here were that she stayed in school and she had an escort wherever she went.

Yohan graciously took the honor of being her lackey. If she ever needed anything, a ride to the store, money, he was at her beck and call. He didn't mind. Secretly, he used the assignment as a way to court her. He'd found her to be cute when she was younger, and as she'd blossomed into a woman, his attraction to her grew. He'd never crossed that line with her until her seventeenth birthday. He respected The Trio too much to take advantage of Krystal when she was just a child.

She'd come to him that night and poured out her heart. Though she hadn't said the words, she'd made it perfectly clear what she felt for him. She also made sure he understood what she wanted, and he was more than happy to oblige. They'd made love for the first time that night, and he'd kept her close to his heart ever since.

Krystal inched her way behind Yohan. She felt like a kid hiding behind her father before being introduced to a roomful of strangers.

"Stop staring at her," Aubrey's wife said as she looked at the eyes all focused on Krystal.

She stood and made her way over to where the couple stood. She opened her arms to Krystal, and the frightened young woman walked into the accepting hug. One by one, the others joined them until they formed a large, comforting circle around her. They all hugged her, touched her, and poured a sense of comfort and belonging over her as she cried.

Having drawn in the comfort from her extended family, Krystal slowly pulled away. She looked around at everyone and she understood what they'd done. They'd shown her what it meant to be a part of this family. No matter what, they'd be there for each other. She was grateful for their comfort, and she'd allow them to help her through this.

Sitting in a recliner, her knees pulled up to her chest, Krystal listened for half an hour as everyone gave their two cents about the best way to help her. She didn't say a word; she just observed each person's unique point of view. Finally, tired of hearing people talk about her situation as if she were invisible, she made her way to the window. The discussion grew intense, keeping everyone's attention so captured that none of them noticed her inching her way across the room, or at least she thought no one noticed.

Though most of his attention had been focused on helping the others decide the best course of action to help Krystal, Yohan kept a watchful eye on her mood. She'd been withdrawn since the discussion began. He'd watched as she edged further away from them, and his concern escalated when she finally got up and walked over to the window. He excused himself from the conversation and made his way over to check on her.

"How you holding up?" Yohan kneaded the tension in her shoulders, hoping to relax her just a little.

Staring out into the darkness, she replied, "It's hard for people to make a decision about another person's life when they really don't know what it is they're dealing with."

"How so?" Yohan didn't quite understand what it was Krystal was trying to tell him.

"You all really don't know."

"I'm not following you."

She turned to face him. Grabbing his hand and pulling him toward the others, she said, "I don't know if I'll be able to repeat this, so I need to say it to everyone."

No one noticed as the couple rejoined the group. Finally, Krystal interrupted the heated discussion with four softly spoken words: "Can I say something?"

An eerie silence fell among them. She leaned back against Yohan's chest, gaining strength from him before speaking. She closed her eyes and said, "Before you come to a decision, there's something you need to know. No matter what you decide, I am willing and ready to face this. But, I think in order for you all to make the best decision, you need to know what I saw that night."

Her eyes closed as she waited for someone to respond. She couldn't look at them. The longer she trapped her vision in darkness, the more vivid the images of the night she'd found Jerad became. She needed the visual when she told her story. It'd guide her through the events on a mental and physical level. The others needed to know what she saw, how she felt, and what she thought in order for them to understand what kind of help she needed.

Yohan wrapped his arms around her, intertwining his fingers with hers. When comfort completely consumed her, she began. "Before I stepped into the apartment, I knew he was dead. . . . When I saw the blood, I didn't know what to think. I kept seeing him there, dead, even though I hadn't opened the door. I tried to think positive, but everything around me was telling me he was gone. . . ."

Krystal relived each painstaking moment of the night of Jerad's death. She told them how she'd found him, lying in a tub full of bloody water. ". . . I just needed to hold him a little while longer. My mind knew he was already gone but my heart just couldn't let go. I couldn't lose him. Not like that. I just couldn't lose him."

By the time she retold the events of the night, she was on the floor in tears. She'd pulled away from Yohan, not allowing him or any of the others to touch her. She needed to experience the pain; she needed to see Jerad's face in her mind; she needed to be in the moment, alone, just as she'd been the night she'd found him dead.

No one said a word. They just listened to what she'd been through. None of them could fathom the hurt and anguish she'd contended with for these last four years. They all wanted so much to help her, to take away the pain, but they didn't know how.

"Take me home." Krystal looked up at Yohan with tears pooling in her eyes. She was on the verge of a serious breakdown, and she didn't want to do it in front of everyone.

Andre was about to tell her she was already home when his girl stopped him. She understood what Krystal meant. Secretly, she'd been watching the relationship between Krystal and Yohan solidify. She knew the girl considered Yohan's home her home. True, she had a room in Andre's house, but it wasn't home anymore.

Krystal reached up for Yohan, allowing him to help her from the floor. He held her close, his best attempt at comforting her. Looking around at all of the people who cared so much for her, none of them able to lift her from the depths of despair, he watched as emotion overwhelmed them all. Without saying a word, he grabbed her things, scooped her into his arms, and carried her out of the apartment.

Chapter Six

"Someone care to explain to me what just happened?" Andre asked in confusion.

Antonio and Aubrey looked at their brother with bewilderment. Surely he'd seen what they'd seen. It should have been easy for him to figure out what was going on between Krystal and Yohan, especially since Krystal lived under his roof.

"Come on, Dre. Don't tell me you haven't figured it out yet," Aubrey replied.

"Figured out what?" He turned in the direction of snickering and asked Kymera, "What are you laughing at?"

"You," she replied. "Even I've figured out they're in love."

Immediately, Andre was on his feet, pacing. "I'll kill him for taking advantage of her." His hands flexed as he tried to control the anger growing inside.

"You will do no such thing." Aubrey needed to snuff the fuse on the time bomb his brother had just become. He'd had the same initial reaction when he'd first realized Krystal's and Yohan's relationship had become more than platonic.

"Dre, come with me." Andre followed his older brother into Krystal's bedroom. "Now take a good look around and tell me what you see."

Dre scanned the room. Everything appeared to be in its place. The bed was neatly made with her stuffed animals lined orderly across the pillows. The curtains were drawn, the closet and bathroom doors were closed, and her computer desk was spotless.

"Am I missing something?"

"Open your eyes, man. Her pictures of her and Jerad are gone, her laptop is missing, and I bet if you look in the closet and dresser drawers you'll see they're nearly empty. Think about it, man. When's the last time Krystal even slept in this bed?"

"Now that you say dat, she hasn't come home at night in a minute. Damn. I can't believe I didn't see this shit sooner."

"Don't beat yourself up. It was destined to happen."

"I just don't want any mishaps. She still got one more year of high school and she's already talking about college."

"We'll make sure she stays on track. In the meantime, we'll have a man-to-man with Yohan, and I'll have the missus talk to Krystal. We'll make sure they're taking the necessary precautions."

"But she's just a baby."

"Come on, Dre. Krystal hasn't been a baby in a long time. Look at it this way: Wouldn't you rather her be with Yohan than some of these other knuckleheads running around here? At least we can still keep tabs on her."

"I guess you're right," he replied, glancing around the room again. "I still don't like it."

"I'm not asking you to. But at the moment, her life needs to remain as normal as possible. He's the one she's depending on. We have bigger problems to deal with, and she's going to need him by her side every step of the way. Besides, whether you realize it or not, they're good

for each other. And with as much time as they spend together, this really shouldn't be a surprise."

Aubrey walked out of the room with Andre trailing
behind. They joined the others in the living room to
make a final decision as to how to help Krystal. Andre,
pouting as usual, silently took a seat on the couch next to
his girl. He still wasn't comfortable with the idea of Krystal and Yohan being a couple, but under the circumstances, he'd let it go for now. He planned to confront
Yohan, but he could wait.

"Back to business. Now that we know the whole story,
what are we going to do about it?" Leave it to Antonio to
get everyone back on track.

"I think you should send her to the woman Yohan
mentioned. Krystal seems more comfortable talking about
this when there are women around. Didn't he say she
was the best in her field?" Aubrey's wife had tried to stay
out of the conversation, but they were getting nowhere.

"I agree. I don't think she'd ever have just told us,"
Antonio replied.

"If no one else has any objections, I think our decision
has been made." Aubrey looked to each person, waiting
for some opposition. When no one made any other sug-
gestions, he said, "Well, I guess that's it. I'll let Yohan
know in the morning."

They all stood, each preparing to make his or her way
back to their respective homes.

"Can I talk to you two in private?" Andre addressed
his brothers as he made his way into the spare bedroom.

Aubrey leaned down and kissed his wife. "I'll be back
in a minute." He followed Antonio into the bedroom and
closed the door behind them.

Walking a narrow path between the bed and the far
wall, Andre said, "We need to talk to Yohan soon. Krystal
has enough to deal with. She doesn't need any added

stress, and she surely doesn't need to face the possibly of getting pregnant."

"I'll talk to him tomorrow when I tell him our decision."

"No!" Dre stared his brother down. "We all need to talk to him."

"What's the difference?"

"Stop it, you two." Antonio intervened, attempting to bring this soon-to-be altercation under control. "I agree with Andre on this one. Yohan needs to clearly understand this is something we're all concerned about."

"Fine. I'll have him meet us at the club Friday night if that's all right with you two." Aubrey's eyes ran up and down his brother. He pursed his lips, choosing to remain civilized under the circumstances.

"I'm cool with that," Dre replied.

"Me too."

"Then I'll see you all Friday." Aubrey left his brothers in the bedroom as he went to get his wife. They needed to get to the babysitter and pick up their children.

A minute or so after he left the bedroom, they heard the front door close.

"You all right, man?" Antonio was concerned about his brother. Aubrey seemed to think that Andre was cool, but he wasn't so sure. Antonio could feel his twin's moods sometimes, and right now he felt the pain Andre held inside.

"What? You think I'm going to fall apart like Krystal did?"

"That's not what I meant and you know it. I know reading that letter was hard. I just wanted to make sure you're good."

"Yeah. I'm straight."

Looking over Andre one last time, Antonio dropped it. "I'll see you Friday."

"Yeah. Whatever."

Antonio understood where Andre's attitude was coming from. He just hoped his brother would deal with his issues.

Chapter Seven

Like every Friday night, people packed into the club like sardines. Yohan sat on the couch in the office watching as Aubrey walked a path in the floor between the matching chairs and the marble-topped desk. He wasn't sure why The Trio had called him here tonight. Aubrey had said something about needing to talk to him, but he'd given no indication as to what this meeting was about.

"There's something we need to address," Aubrey began as he turned off the big-screen television, leaving an eerie hush floating among them.

Andre leaned back in the chair behind the desk, his fingers intertwined behind his head, his eyes narrowed, staring at Yohan. The cigar smoke he expelled billowed like a cartoon rain cloud above his head before disappearing in the suction of the vents near the ceiling. Antonio sat in the leather chair to Yohan's right, his left ankle resting on the opposite knee, his arms crossed over his chest. Never before had Yohan seen such underlying anger and distrust hovering beneath the surface of Antonio's light brown eyes.

Uneasiness crept up Yohan's spine as he watched the expressions of his comrades. If he didn't know any better, he'd swear he was a rat cornered by a dancing cobra waiting, taunting, preparing to strike. However, unlike the rat, Yohan didn't know what the outcome of his current situation entailed. He waited patiently under unwavering scrutiny for Aubrey to address whatever concern The Trio had.

"For the past four years, we've watched your relationship with Krystal evolve. We've stood on the sidelines, allowing nature to take its course. But Yohan, we want to caution you. We understand right now Krystal's life needs to remain as stable as possible; however, we've been watching what's going on between you two and some aspects have as of late become"—he stopped for a moment, contemplating the right word—"concerning."

"Quit dancing around it, Brey!" Andre smacked his palms on the desktop as he stood. "Are you two fucking?"

"I don't think that's any of your business," Yohan snapped back, not believing his sexual life with Krystal was being questioned.

"Dre!" The sound of his name halted the word his lips had already formed. Antonio turned to his twin with an unspoken threat in his eyes. The last thing they needed was to have Yohan on the defensive. They'd only agreed to do this to insure the couple was using protection, not to create a wedge in their relationship.

"Look, Yohan, unlike Dre, Aubrey and I could care less whether or not you and Krystal are sleeping together. As far as we're concerned, you're both mature adults. However, in keeping with Krystal's best interests, we just want to make sure that if you two are having sex, you're taking the necessary precautions to prevent any 'accidents.'"

Yohan closed his eyes, thinking through his response. Though he and Krystal had discussed telling the Trio how they felt, they hadn't taken the time to realize the possibility that their actions may have already given them away. He loved her, and he wasn't ashamed of that; he just wished he'd said something before things came to this.

Opening his eyes, Yohan looked at each of them before speaking. Aubrey appeared to be his usual self, waiting patiently for his response. Antonio showed no outward sign of emotion other than a relaxed posture and facial expression. Lastly, Yohan rested his gaze on Andre. Dre's reaction to his relationship with Krystal was most concerning.

Since the first day Krystal came to Lincoln Heights, Andre was always protective of her. The last two years, though, he'd paid less attention, mainly because she was growing up and becoming more independent. Not only that; he had more to tend to in his life with taking over most of the responsibilities of the garage and his ongoing relationship. Still, this sudden concern of his troubled Yohan.

Yohan's gaze never wavered from Andre's as he began, "I'm going to put aside the fact that as a twenty-one-year-old man I don't owe any of you an explanation. But, Krystal and I have spoken at length about what it is she wants. We've talked about her future plans, and those plans still include her going to college. We've discussed family life and where she sees herself in three to five years, and although I've encouraged her to date other people, she continues to voice her love and commitment to me.

"I only want what's best for her, and that includes insuring she gets her education before having any children. I've left the decision of birth control pills up to her, but I make sure we use a condom every time."

Yohan returned Andre's glare, indicating he had no intentions of backing down. His love life with Krystal was none of their business, but he'd told them enough, he hoped, to diminish any possible concerns they may have had regarding his commitment to what was best for her.

Aubrey grabbed Andre before he lunged at Yohan. He'd watched the staring match between the two. Yohan was patient; he'd wait for Andre to make the first move. Dre, on the other hand, would consider Yohan's death stare a sign of disrespect and he'd take it personally.

"Don't even think about it," Aubrey said to his brother through gritted teeth.

"Yohan, will you excuse us?" Antonio said, making his way over to where Aubrey had Andre pinned to the wall.

Only Andre watched Yohan exit the office. When the sound of the latch catching signaled his departure, Aubrey let Dre go.

"Now, what is your problem?" Aubrey asked.

"He is not going to disrespect me like that!" Dre forced the chair against the wall. He wanted to throw something, punch a wall, do anything to let the anger out.

"And what exactly did he just do to disrespect you?" Aubrey remained calm, hoping his mood would rub off on his brother.

"You saw the way he was trying to stare me down like I'm some punk on the street."

"Last time I checked, you started it."

"Come on, Dre," Antonio interrupted. "We all know that's not the problem." Antonio decided to draw the focus away from Andre's excuse back to the truth at hand. Nothing would change until Andre admitted to himself what was really bothering him.

"Okay, Mr. All-Knowing, tell me what my problem is."

"Oh, I'll tell you what your problem is, but the real question here is, are you really ready to hear and deal with it?"

"Oh, I'm ready. I'm sure this is going to be good." Andre plopped down in the leather chair across from Antonio. Aubrey claimed the vacant space on the couch as they waited for Antonio to enlighten them.

"Your problem is simple enough. You're acting like any father would toward his daughter's boyfriends. Not only that, in your eyes, Krystal is still Jerad's woman. That means Yohan is sleeping with Jerad's woman. Therein lies your problem."

"Whatever," was all Andre could say.

"Are you denying that's your problem?"

Andre stood and made his way over to the two-way mirror, turning his back on his brothers.

"Dre, sooner or later you're going to have to let her go. Jerad didn't want her to spend the rest of her life alone. She's found happiness. Can't you for once put aside the fact she was once Jerad's woman and be happy for her?"

Andre didn't respond. Instead, for the remainder of the night he stood at the mirror, staring out into the crowd. What Antonio said had hit close to home. He did still see her as Jerad's woman and he needed to deal with that.

Both Antonio and Aubrey understood how hard this was on him. Antonio only wanted his brother to accept that Jerad would always have a special place in Krystal's heart, but she was taking steps to get on with her life, and he needed to do the same.

Krystal relaxed as the warm Jacuzzi water massaged her back. She, Yquira, and Kymera had spent most of the afternoon getting pampered. They'd decided that since the guys were having a guys' night out, they'd have a girls' night out.

The women sat in opposite corners of the eldest Fedichi's Jacuzzi relaxing, enjoying the time away from their men. They'd had a good day, but Krystal still had the feeling that there was an ulterior motive for this girls' night out.

"Krystal, can we talk to you about something?"

She turned in the direction of the lady of the house. "I knew it. So what is it? The drug speech? Staying in school? What am I going to do with my life?"

"Actually, the guys wanted us to talk to you about birth control."

Krystal twisted her lips in a not so pleasant scowl.

"They're just concerned. They want to make sure if you and Yohan are having sex that you're using protection."

"Look, neither of us is ready to start a family; he uses a condom every time."

"Have you thought about birth control pills? I mean, the more protection the better. Condoms do break. Believe me, I know." Aubrey's wife giggled the minute the word escaped. Their newborn was the result of a broken condom.

"Yeah, but I hate taking medicine." Krystal shook her head, still not believing that tonight had been a setup. She should have known something was up—everybody was being way too nice.

"There are other options." The lady of the house gave her a serious but understanding look.

"I know. We discussed all of them in graphic detail. He even took me to a gynecologist and brought home handfuls of pamphlets. I swear I was in a sex education class that night."

"He didn't!"

"He did." They all laughed, now knowing the lengths Yohan had gone to make sure they were making an informed decision. He really did love Krystal and his actions were always in her best interest.

"Do you have any other questions? I mean, you can't exactly learn everything from doctors, books, and pamphlets."

"Well, I do have some, but they're not birth-control related." Her cheeks turned pink, and though she tried, the smile inching its way across her face clearly showed the thoughts bouncing around her mind.

The two other women exchanged glances. They knew what kind of questions Krystal had and they were more than willing to tell her all they'd learned over the years.

"We'd better get out of the Jacuzzi. This is going to take some time."

The three of them climbed from the warm water and after taking a few minutes to dry off, they gathered around the patio furniture to have their powwow.

"So where do we start? Foreplay or technique?" Aubrey's wife asked.

Krystal knew exactly where she wanted to start. "Definitely foreplay."

For the remainder of the night, the three women sat in the wicker furniture beneath the stars discussing everything from biology to the euphoria of orgasms. Krystal learned some new tricks that she couldn't wait to try with Yohan. And though somewhat disturbing, she learned some interesting bedroom habits of the men who tried to protect her from everything.

Chapter Eight

Krystal's locker creaked on its hinges as she swung the door open. It felt weird to be back at school. The words from Jerad's letter still floated through her mind like the letters in alphabet soup. She was hoping to make it through the day, but Yohan had told her if she felt she couldn't do it to just call.

Looking down at her now-healing hands, the scabs reminded her of the breakdown she'd had only five days earlier. Releasing a breath, she slid her books from her backpack into the emptiness of the locker. As she reached for the notebook for her first class, a looming presence at her back drew her attention.

"Word out is you know that hunk of dark chocolate that was in the office the other day."

Krystal recognized the voice. Her first day back at school and drama was already finding her. "So what if I do?" she replied, not taking the time to turn around and look the school bully, Sherri, in the face.

Sherri McMillian stood at six feet one with long, slender legs. She kept her hair cropped short and feathered and the fluorescent lights of the hall always flickered across her golden highlights. She was what Southerners referred to as *red-boned*. Although she was pleasant to the eyes, Sherri proclaimed herself the roughest girl in school. She ruled by intimidation and for years, no one dared challenge her. However, Sherri picked on those she deemed lesser than her. By most accounts, Krystal was considered a nerd and kept to herself. And as cocaptain of the varsity cheerleading squad, she remained off of Sherri's list of victims.

"I think dark chocolate and vanilla go well together. Don't you?" Sherri ran her hand over her slender figure, taking care to give a little shimmy to the guy gawking at her.

"Whatever." Krystal busied her hands, rummaging through her purse for her makeup case. She so didn't feel like being bothered with Sherri today, and especially if she was interested in Yohan.

"So how about you hook a sister up?"

Krystal stopped in mid-swipe of her gloss. She looked in the mirror hung in her locker at the girl who'd just asked for the hookup with her boyfriend.

"He's already spoken for," she replied, rolling her eyes and continuing the application of her lip gloss.

"So," Sherri stated. "Once he gets a taste of this rich vanilla, he'll drop the bitch he's with now."

"First of all"—Krystal turned around to stare Sherri dead in her eyes—"you don't know a damn thing about Yohan. Secondly, you need to watch who you calling a bitch, bitch."

Sherri looked Krystal up and down, sizing her up one good time before she made her move. Then, drawing back, she swung. The impact of Sherri's fist with Krystal's jaw didn't faze her. She and Yohan boxed every other weekend, so she knew how to take a punch. Compared to some of the blows Yohan landed when they play fought, Sherri's hit was light.

Krystal's tongue licked the spot on her lip where she felt the blood dripping. "Nice," she said as she reached with her right hand to wipe away the blood trailing down her chin.

Sherri stared at Krystal, gloating, proud of the blow she'd delivered but confused as to why it hadn't taken the girl down. She was so absorbed in her personal pride and Krystal wiping the blood from her lip that she never saw the left hook coming. Before she had time to react, Krystal swiped Sherri's feet from under her. Her body hit the floor with a thud. Krystal delivered three swift kicks to Sherri's midsection before resting her foot on the girl's throat.

A crowd had formed in the hallway, now surrounding them on all sides. The students cheered Krystal on as someone finally stood up to Sherri.

"Now, bitch, you got some other name to call me?"

Sherri didn't get the chance to answer. One of the teachers grabbed Krystal while one of the nuns helped a bent-over and bleeding Sherri from the cold, blood-stained tile floor.

Krystal held the ice pack the nurse gave her securely against her busted lip. She rolled her eyes and let out a disconcerting sigh as the office door swung open and Aubrey stomped in. He cut his eyes at her, showing his displeasure at having to climb out of bed early in the morning after a long night at the club.

"What did you do?" he asked.

"Nothing you wouldn't approve of," Krystal replied with a sneer, trying her best not to look him in the face.

The Trio only resorted to violence in the most extreme of cases. She knew Aubrey was mad. His anger was plastered over his face like a warrior's mask. She paid it no mind. Once the principal explained to him that she was only defending herself, his anger would dissipate and turn to compassion.

"Mr. Fedichi, you sure are spending a lot of your time here. Have a seat."

Aubrey claimed the seat next to Krystal. She turned away, hoping he wouldn't ask to see her lip. He caught the gesture and turned her to face him.

"Let me see the damage."

She lowered the ice pack, revealing her split lip and slightly swollen jaw.

"Who were you fighting with?"

"The school bully." She smacked her lips and rolled her eyes.

"What for?"

"Look, I just defended myself. She hit me first."

"Did you provoke her?" Aubrey had warned Krystal about her smart mouth. He'd told her sooner or later that mouth of hers was going to write a check her ass couldn't cover. By the looks of her lip, his prediction had finally come to pass.

"If you think me telling her no when she asked for the hookup with Yohan is 'provoking' her, then yeah. Besides, she called me a bitch, and you know I don't play that shit. If I don't let a man call me a bitch, I damn sho' ain't gonna let no light-skinned heifer call me one."

"Watch your mouth, young lady."

"Mr. Fedichi," a voice from behind the desk called, "you can go in now."

Aubrey watched as a tall, thin girl with a black eye and bruised cheek walked past with a woman he assumed was her mother. The girl mouthed something at Krystal he couldn't quite make out. Apparently Krystal understood the words because she responded by mouthing *bring it on*.

"Krystal." Aubrey cut the silent conversation short. She was already in enough trouble.

"Aubrey Fedichi. I haven't seen you in the principal's office since your senior year when you and the captain of the football team tipped over a set of bleachers on the football field."

Aubrey laughed as he remembered how easy the stunt had been. "Yeah, it has been a long time. So what do you make of this situation with Krystal?"

"From what we've gathered from the students who witnessed the fight, Miss McMillian threw the first blow." The man leaned forward, resting his elbows on the desk. "Krystal was just defending herself. We're still going to have to suspend her, though."

"How many days is she looking at?" Aubrey leaned back in the chair, still not quite sure what to make of this situation.

"Ten. Since Krystal is such an exemplary student, I'll make arrangements with her instructors to make sure she doesn't fall behind in her classes."

"I appreciate that. Who was the girl she was fighting?"

"Actually, she *was* the school bully." The principal stressed the word *was*. "We've been trying to get her out of here for a long time. This little fight with Miss Bao just sealed the deal."

"Well, thanks again." Aubrey stood, preparing to leave when the principal stopped him.

"May I ask you a question?" The man tapped the end of his pen on a notepad, a clear indication of his nervousness.

Aubrey's expression relaxed and he revealed a smirk before replying, "Sure."

"I was surprised to see you here checking on Krystal. Her last name isn't Fedichi." He raised an eyebrow, waiting for the eldest Fedichi to respond.

"I'm just her legal guardian." Aubrey turned and quickly exited the office. He didn't need the principal asking questions about how he came to be Krystal's legal guardian. They'd forged the documents to get her into school, and the last thing he needed right now was someone starting to question them.

"Let's go, young lady." Aubrey headed toward the door, pausing for only a moment to wait for Krystal to gather her things. As they walked down the empty halls, he said, "You do know that these ten days aren't going to be days off for you, right?"

"What's that supposed to mean?" Krystal adjusted her bag as they stepped outside.

"I think someone needs a lesson in responsibility." Aubrey opened the passenger side door and allowed Krystal to climb in.

"I have the feeling I'm not going to like this." Aubrey never tolerated insubordination, and she'd done just that with this little scuffle in the halls.

"You might not, but I think the missus will enjoy her time away from the little one. I know what a little demon my son can be at times."

Aubrey closed the door as he rounded the car to the driver's side. Ten school days having to babysit his son should give Krystal incentive enough to think twice before acting out in school.

Chapter Nine

Krystal dashed into the bedroom, snatching the ring-ing phone from the cradle.

"Hey," China replied to her greeting. "I've been ring-ing this bell for ten minutes. Come open the door."

"I was in the tub. Be there in a sec." Sliding on a terry-cloth robe and tying it at the waist, Krystal headed for the front door. She remembered Yohan saying good-bye as he headed out to run some errands. She wasn't expect-ing China for another half an hour, so she'd decided to take a bath.

Standing behind the door, she opened it, allowing China to enter her quaint little home.

"Hurry up! Close the door." China rushed past Krystal as quickly as the extra load she carried would allow.

"What's up?"

"There's this creepy guy in the parking lot." China car-ried one overly stuffed backpack over her shoulder while dragging in another. She clutched at the stack of folders, which threatened to slip from her grasp and plunge into one large, messy pile at her feet. "You could help, you know."

Krystal gathered the loose articles from her friend. She used her hip to shut the door. She grabbed the bag China had slung over her shoulder and carried it to the couch. "Do I need to call in reinforcements?"

"You might want to let Yohan know. He's light-skinned, wearing jeans, a white T-shirt, and some blue and white Timbs."

Krystal grabbed the phone and relayed the message to Yohan. He told her he was only ten minutes away and he'd be there as soon as possible. In the meantime, he'd call the guys and give them the heads-up.

Hanging up the phone, Krystal turned her attention to the stack of folders and her book bag. "So I guess this is all of my homework?"

"Yep. You'd better be glad I had the combination to your locker. The least they could have done was let you get your books."

"You know how Aubrey is. He couldn't wait to lecture me about the fight. If he hadn't been so mad, I probably would have had the chance to get my things. Did you grab my makeup case?"

"Right here." China tossed the leopard print case to her friend. "Girl, they have been talking about you at school all day long."

Hand on hip, she asked, "Do I really want to know what people are saying?"

"Most of it's good."

"Let me put on some clothes and you can tell me all about it. Are you going to do my hair tonight?" Krystal walked in the direction of the back hallway. Her pace slowed just enough to give China a chance to respond to her question.

"I can if you want. Do you have the needle and the hair?"

"Sure do. I'll be back in a minute."

Krystal entered the bedroom she shared with Yohan. She grabbed a T-shirt and a pair of pajama pants and slipped them on. Unwrapping the scarf tied around her head, she plucked the bag of hair from the chair, took the comb, needle, and thread from the bathroom drawer and joined China in the living room.

"Here." She tossed the bag to her friend before sliding down onto the floor. Pressing the guide button on the remote, she surfed through the hundreds of channels, finding nothing of interest.

With her head tilted down, China combed through her locks.

"So what's the scoop?"

"Girl, let me tell you. You are damn near a goddess in that place. Everybody's talking about how you gave Sherri the straight beat-down. We all knew one day she was gonna pick on the wrong one, but none of us expected it to be you."

"Guess their mamas never taught them. It's the quiet ones you got to watch out for."

"Yeah, she never saw that one coming." China finished the first braid and started sewing in the first track of hair. "But you know her crew kinda mad."

"I am so not worried about them. Without Sherri, they'll eventually fall apart." Krystal stopped on a music channel. She turned the volume down and handed the remote to China.

"I hope so. Word out is they planning to jump you after school when you get back. But nobody thinks they can pull it off. Besides, everybody's on your side. If one of them so much as steps out of line, they'll have to deal with the cheerleaders, football team, basketball players, along with the teachers. Girl, even some of the nuns got your back."

"I kinda wished I hadn't gotten her expelled, though. Where you think she going now?"

"Don't know, and to tell you the truth, don't care. She got what she deserved—a royal ass-kicking. And you didn't get her expelled. She's been on her way out of that place since she got there."

"But now she's going to be terrorizing some other school."

"Better them than us." China pulled at Krystal's hair, attempting to slide the needle through. Apparently, she'd braided the center part a little too tight.

"If you say so. Ouch! Watch what you doing up there."

"My bad." She rubbed her finger over the spot she'd just pulled the needle through. "It doesn't look like your head is bleeding."

"It'd better not be."

Krystal relaxed a little, knowing that her classmates felt safer. She truly felt bad for Sherri getting kicked out of school. But what China said was true. Only Sherri could be blamed for her situation.

"I know we haven't really talked since the other day, but I wanted to ask how's my girl doing." Lately, China's concern for her friend was hitting maximum meltdown.

"What do you mean, how am I doing? I'm doing fine, just like I've always been."

"Fine, huh. You didn't look fine when you walked out of that classroom nearly in tears. And don't think I didn't notice the cuts on your hands. I've been where you are, Krystal. I know what happens when you feel like you just can't do it anymore."

"So I guess you're going to start too. Why can't y'all

just understand that I can handle this?" She tried to move, but the tugging on her hair made her think twice.

"Stop lying to yourself. We all need help sometimes."

"Well, I'm getting help. Now, can we talk about something else?" She wanted to get up and walk away, but she didn't want to be stabbed in the head again, so she stayed put.

"Sure."

China allowed Krystal to steer the conversation in a more cheerful direction. She understood that her friend was taking things day by day. She just hoped Krystal had told the truth. She didn't want to lose her best friend.

Chapter Ten

Yohan rounded the corner, making his usual rounds through Lincoln Heights, seeing who was skipping school, when he ran across an unfamiliar face. He'd deliver the two sets of rims he'd picked up during his morning runs, and he didn't need to be at the club for the morning supply delivery for at least another hour or so. He rolled to a stop in front of the teenaged boy sitting on the stoop of one of the apartment buildings. "Hey, young buck, what you doing down here?"

"I *was* minding my own business." The boy took a drag from his cigarette and flicked the butt into the bushes.

Yohan kept his thoughts to himself. He threw the truck in park, grabbed his pistol, and climbed out of the vehicle. The young boy stood as he approached. He couldn't have been more than five feet nine, a hundred fifty, hundred sixty pounds at most, nearly a foot shorter and seventy pounds lighter than his soon-to-be adversary.

Yohan towered over the now frightened teenager. His size alone was intimidating, and with the chrome .357 in his left hand, he was downright terrifying. "Smart-alecky comments like that are why you can't be nice to people. Now, answer my question."

"I don't want no trouble." The boy upheld both hands so this man could see he didn't have a weapon. "I just got tired of my moms ragging on me 'cause I ain't got no job."

"You live around here?" Yohan glared at the boy, frightening him even more.

"Yeah. Me and my moms just moved in upstairs."

"What's your name?"

"Nigel." He relaxed a little, hoping that this wasn't going to turn into a petty robbery or worse.

"Well, Nigel," Yohan holstered his weapon, "I guess I should welcome you to Lincoln Heights. Since you're new around here, there are a few people you should meet. Got any plans tonight?"

"No. Why?" Nigel took in the man before him. He was clean-cut, muscular. He appeared to know how to handle his weapon. If this guy was any indication of the rest of the neighbors, he thought he might need to watch himself.

"Play poker?" Yohan asked.

"A little."

"Meet me at ten-sixty-eight around seven. It's the last building on your right near the back of the complex. Think you can manage that?"

Nigel stepped back and looked over the man standing before him, trying to decide whether or not to trust him.

"Don't worry. We don't bite. Kill, maybe, but never bite. And who knows, maybe you'll even leave with a job. Just think about it." Yohan turned and made his way back to his vehicle. Climbing into the driver's seat, he watched the youngster again take a seat on the stoop. As he pulled off, he wondered if Nigel would show up tonight.

Picking up his phone, Yohan dialed Andre's number. He needed to warn The Trio they'd have company tonight.

"Whadup?" Andre asked, his words slurring together into one short phrase.

"Just called to let you know we might have a visitor tonight." He cut the corner close. The sound of a tree branch scraping his paint job caused his nose to bunch up and his face to turn to a frown.

"Anyone we know?"

"Probably not. Kid says him and his moms just moved in." He stopped short, flipping one of the guys on the basketball court a bird.

"Is he gonna be trouble?"

"If we can get him on the right path, I don't think so. He says his moms been ragging him about not having a job. I figured once you guys got a feel for him maybe you'd be able to help him out."

"I'll call Brey and Tonio and let them know."

The sound of the dial tone rang in Yohan's ear as he pulled into his parking space. He started to get out, then decided to take a ride. For some reason, he just didn't feel like going into the house. He needed to be outside and he knew just the place to quench his thirst for adventure. Pulling back out of the parking space, he headed in the direction of his favorite spot, an outdoor shooting range nestled in the confines of Lithonia.

Yohan handed Andre a glass of Hennessy on the rocks. For the last hour, they'd watched Antonio deliver beating after beating to Aubrey in *Halo 2*. Sometimes they wondered how much time that boy spent with his fingers glued to the Xbox.

"I don't think your boy is going to show," Andre said.

Yohan looked over at the small antique cuckoo clock

sitting on the mantle. Krystal saw it at an antique show and after ten minutes of giving him puppy-dog eyes, he finally broke down and bought it for her. She giggled every time she watched the little bird peep his head out the tiny doors. The clock read five minutes to seven.

"He'll show. Besides, these two,"—He gestured toward the guys on the couch—"don't look anywhere near ready to move from the television to the table."

"Aye, say the word and I'm done. I don't think I can take much more of this." Aubrey's fingers and thumbs continued to pound the buttons on the controller as his brother's score surpassed his.

Just then, the doorbell rang. Yohan turned to Andre, delivering a smug, "Told you so."

Two hours and fifteen hands later, the five men stared at their cards. The sweet scent of vanilla and pina colada cigar smoke filled the room and two empty Heinekens and one empty Hennessy bottle sat in a pile on the floor.

"I fold," Nigel proclaimed, throwing his cards in the middle of the table.

"Me too." Andre tossed his three cards into the discard pile forming in front of Yohan.

"Which one of y'all dealt me this shit? I'm out." Antonio grabbed his beer and waited for Yohan and Aubrey to decide what they were going to do.

"Well, Brey, looks like it's just you and me."

"I'll raise you,"—Aubrey dropped ten dollars into the mound of money in the center of the table—"and call. Put up or shut up."

"Straight." Yohan laid the eight of spades, nine of clubs, and ten of diamonds in a spread on the table.

All eyes turned to Aubrey. Three-card poker was his specialty. He was master of the blank stare. Antonio only had enough money left for a couple more games, and Andre was in worse shape than his twin. Yohan, though, had gotten a couple of lucky hands. He was the only one able to keep up with Aubrey tonight. Even the newbie hadn't caught a break.

"Mighty pretty hand you got right there. Too bad it can't compete with my three lovely ladies. Read 'em and weep, boys."

"Daaaamn. How does he do that?" Yohan asked, watching Aubrey collect the last of the pool money.

"We've been trying to figure that out for years," Antonio joked.

Before Yohan finished shuffling the cards to deal the next hand, the front door swung open. Krystal and China sashayed into the living room, breaking their conversation only long enough to acknowledge the people in the room.

"Hi, boys," Krystal teased as she followed her friend into one of the back bedrooms.

"Daaaamn. I wouldn't mind having that ass in my bed," Nigel exclaimed as he watched Krystal enter the bedroom and close the door behind her.

Everyone else froze. The room became so quiet they heard the water dripping from the faucet in the kitchen. Aubrey, Andre, and Antonio exchanged glances as they inched away from the table. Nigel had just crossed the line. Although The Trio treated Krystal like a sister, they allowed Yohan to handle most business concerning her.

As Nigel turned around to look at his hand, his eyes met with the barrel of a .357.

"Let me explain something to you," Yohan began in a voice too calm for the situation. "In Lincoln Heights, loyalty means everything. The crew takes care of its own no matter what. However, there are a few instances that take precedence over loyalty. I'm only going to say this once. That one is off limits. You stay away from her or I'll personally see to it you reach an early grave. Am I making myself clear?"

"Crystal."

Yohan lowered his weapon, sliding it back into the holster.

"My bad, man." Nigel threw his hands up in a sign of surrender. "I didn't mean any disrespect."

"Just so we're clear."

The Trio returned to the table, proud of how Yohan had handled the situation. They knew how much Krystal meant to him, and his actions confirmed their assumption that no matter what, he'd do whatever it took to protect her.

Chapter Eleven

A cool, crisp breeze swept Krystal's hair from her face. She'd spent most of the morning on the balcony of the apartment she shared with Yohan. She'd completed most of the homework China had brought her, so the remainder of the day consisted of watching Aubrey's youngest.

Yohan waved good-bye as he pulled out of his parking spot to make his rounds. His morning runs consisted of running to suppliers to pick up inventory for both of the auto repair shops and the club. After that he'd be the Trio's go-fer, running any errands that anyone needed during the day up until it was time to pick her up from school. Rounds normally took a couple of hours, so she had plenty of time to figure out what to do with the rest of the day.

When he was no longer in her range of vision, she reentered the sanctuary of their bedroom. Glancing around the room, ensuring everything was in order, she decided to take little man to the neighborhood park. She slid his tiny arms into the sleeves of his jacket and, grabbing a blanket and a book, scooped the little one into her arms as she headed for the neighborhood park.

A few minutes of rocking and singing and baby boy's yawns turned into a sound sleep. Krystal laid him on the blanket beside her, watching him curl into the fetal position and slide his thumb into his mouth. Once convinced he was resting peacefully, she lost herself in her book.

A gentleman sitting in a red Dodge Durango slid down in his seat as Yohan drove past. He thought for a moment to follow, but the young woman moving back into the apartment drew his attention. He waited, remaining out of sight until she passed his truck, carrying a young child toward the park area.

With a safe distance between them, the man climbed from his vehicle and followed behind her, taking extra care not to be seen. His head peeped around the corner of one of the buildings as she placed the small child on the blanket next to her. He stood there, observing her, the way the wind brushed her hair against her cheeks, the delicate way she held the book as she read, the gentle care she took when she turned the pages. He wondered what it would feel like to have her fingers caressing his body just as they caressed the paper.

What am I thinking? She's just a child and my ticket to the big payday. Placing one foot in front of the other, he made his way over to where this angel sat.

"Zora Neale Hurston, good choice," he said, leaning against the very tree shading the young girl and the child. Getting a good look at the baby, he took notice that the child didn't resemble the young lady or Yohan.

Krystal turned at the voice she didn't recognize. "Can I help you?" she asked, scooping the sleeping baby into her arms just in case she needed to run.

"Cute kid." He gestured toward the infant.

"Thanks." She stared at the man, burning an image of his face into her mind for safekeeping.

"Look." He observed her change in demeanor. He didn't mean her any harm, but she obviously didn't like him being there. "I was just admiring your beauty and decided to come and introduce myself. My name's Octavio." He reached a hand out to her. She hesitated and then shook it.

"I'm Krystal." She relaxed a little, now having at least a first name to attach to the face. "I haven't seen you around. Did you just move in?" She slid her hand from his and used it to help lift her and the little one's weight from the ground.

"No, I'm here visiting some friends."

"Oh," she replied, shifting the little one's weight to a more comfortable position.

"I've got some business I need to tend to." He reached into his pocket and scribbled a number on a piece of paper. He handed it to her, saying, "I'd love to get to know you. Give me a call sometime." He didn't give her the opportunity to respond; he just turned and walked back toward the building.

Krystal's eyes wandered over the man's backside as the handsome stranger rounded the corner out of her sight. As she turned her attention back to the little one now squirming in her arms, she caught a glimpse of a face she thought she vaguely recognized. The young man quickly darted around the corner in the same direction Octavio had gone. Not thinking anything else of it, Krystal gathered the rest of her belongings and made her way back to the apartment.

"I was wondering where you'd snuck off to," Yohan said, smiling at his woman as she walked through the door.

"I needed a change of scenery, so we went to the park."

She dropped the blanket and her book onto the table by the front door.

"Did you two have a nice time?" Yohan folded the newspaper, giving her his full attention.

"We sure did, didn't we?" She tickled the infant under the chin before handing him to Yohan. "I'd better get cleaned up for my appointment."

"You're really ready for this, aren't you?" Yohan stood the little boy on his knees, making faces and taking joy from making the little one laugh.

"Yeah." She smiled at him. "I think I am."

A sense of warm happiness filled the therapist's office. Though she didn't know why, Krystal expected a more businesslike and less homey atmosphere. Instead of the bland white walls, she found a well-lit office painted in a pastel yellow. Artwork depicting white sandy beaches and flowers hung on the wall behind the pine desk. She moved around the office, stopping in front of a vase holding a spray of flowers she'd never seen before.

"Bird-of-paradise," a soft but confident female voice spoke.

Krystal turned to see the face of a mocha-skinned, slender woman with endless legs. She didn't speak; she just stared at the woman's cropped auburn hair.

"The flowers. They're called bird-of-paradise."

Krystal turned again to look down upon the floral arrangement. Moments later, she turned teary eyes to Yohan. When they'd left the house, she was so sure she was ready for this. Now, though, standing in this cheery place, all of the thoughts of Jerad resurfacing, she wasn't sure.

"It's okay," Yohan said softly, pulling her into his arms. He looked around at the doctor, not quite knowing what to say. She just nodded at him. She understood. The first step was always difficult for the patient.

A few minutes later, when Krystal was sure she'd regained her composure, she pulled away from Yohan. He intertwined his fingers with hers and led her to the chairs placed in front of the doctor's desk.

"Would you like something to drink?" she asked, directing the question at Krystal.

"No, ma'am." Her eyes remained in her hands. Yohan covered hers with his in an attempt to calm her nerves.

"And who is this gentleman with you?"

"My boyfriend." Her response came across timid.

"Well, it's nice to meet you both." The woman scribbled something on her notepad before she looked up at them.

"So, what brings you to see me this afternoon?"

Yohan sat quietly watching Krystal. She needed to own up to this. For too long, they'd protected her, but in doing so, they'd allowed her to keep the pain inside. Now she needed to take that first step, and if she was truly ready, she'd take it on her own.

A long silence hovered in the office. Yohan closed his eyes, secretly praying for Krystal to answer the doctor's question. He bit his bottom lip to keep words from escaping. He kept telling himself this was up to her. If she wasn't strong enough to take the first step, he wasn't sure where this left them.

"A little over four years ago, I found my first love dead. . . ."

For the next hour, Krystal attempted to explain what she'd been through. She danced around the graphic details of that night, choosing to focus on his letter and her feelings toward his words. ". . . so I guess I'm here trying to figure out how to deal with all of this."

"And why is he here?" the doctor asked, gesturing in Yohan's direction.

Krystal faced the man who meant the world to her, a smile threatening to take over her lips. "Sometimes I ask myself the same question. The only answer I've ever come up with is that he's always been here. I've always found it easy to talk to him. Yohan has been by my side since I came here. Even when I make bad choices, he's there to help me pick up the pieces."

"And I always will be," he responded, staring down into her now puffy red eyes.

"I just have a couple of additional questions and then we'll be finished for the day. You mentioned a deeply rooted loss of hope. Have you ever considered suicide?"

Krystal lowered her eyes and then her head. She should have known the doctor would ask. Besides the fact that she'd found Jerad all of those years ago, there was one additional secret she kept from Yohan.

"Yes," she replied in a barely audible voice.

Yohan's eyes grew wide at the confession.

"Have you ever attempted suicide?"

Again Krystal answered, "Yes."

"Do you feel at this moment you're a threat to yourself?"

Krystal shifted in her seat, uncomfortable with the line of questioning. She really didn't know what she felt right now. So many thoughts raced through her mind, some happy, some not so happy, and others still she couldn't quite decipher.

"Krystal, do you think you're a threat to yourself?"

She looked up at the doctor and told her the truth. "I don't know."

Chapter Twelve

As the sun made its final descent, Krystal nestled comfortably in Yohan's arms. Her fingers tightened around the orange prescription bottle she'd gotten from the doctor's office.

"I'm sorry, Yohan," she said, her hand lifting to wipe the tears from her eyes. She hated to feel this way. She hated that everything felt like it was going wrong when she should be having the best years of her life.

"Sorry about what?" He twirled a lock of her hair around his finger. She'd been nearly silent since they'd gotten the medicine, and he'd held her in his arms since they'd gotten in the house.

"I should have told you about—"

"Don't say it. I understand. We all have our demons." He had his as well, but he was better equipped to deal with his.

"You shouldn't have found out like this."

"Don't worry about it. I know you have your reasons for holding on to things. I know sometimes you keep things inside, and I respect that." Respect and like were two different things. He needed for her to face her past. She needed to face her past. The big challenge was how to help her open up.

"Thank you." The only two words she allowed her mouth to say.

Silence hung between them as Krystal tried to decide whether to take the medicine. Yohan left the decision up to her, and regardless of what she chose, he planned to help her through this. Besides, he too had some decisions to make.

"Krystal?" He tilted his head back, resting it against the headboard.

"Yeah."

"I want to ask you something, and I need you to tell me the truth."

She wondered what was on his mind. She speculated, but his request for complete honestly concerned her. "What?"

He pulled her closer, securing her in his arms. For a moment, he wasn't even sure he really wanted to ask the question taunting his mind. If she answered no, he was sure he'd be relieved; however, if she answered yes . . . He needed to know. One way or the other, he had to know.

"Since you've been here, have you ever thought about . . ." He couldn't bring himself to finish the question. If she said yes, everything between them would change, and not necessarily for the better.

He didn't need to finish the question. She understood what he desired to know. When the doctor started asking the question, she was sure this conversation awaited. She was prepared to tell him the truth if that was what he really wanted to know.

"Before I answer, what difference does it make? What's in the past is in the past."

"If that's so true, why are we here? If you've truly left the past in the past, why do you cry in your sleep? You know, you talk to him in your dreams, sometimes for hours during the night. If the past is so much in the past, then why does it haunt you so?"

Krystal reached over and opened the nightstand drawer. She pulled a neatly folded piece of purple stationery from the drawer and handed it to him without responding to his questions.

"I think you need to see this before I answer your question. I wrote it a couple of years after Jerad died, a couple of years after I came here. Whenever I thought about him, I read this and remembered. This is how I felt, and this is how I've dealt with this alone for this long."

Yohan unfolded the piece of paper and stared at the words.

Death don't come knocking at my door too often
It doesn't have to. It has its own key
It lets itself in whenever it sees fit
And it leaves whenever it chooses
You see, Death is my suitor
A welcome squatter in the solitude of these four walls

The shadow stands outside my window
It never looks up at me
But it feels me watching
No, the shadow just stares out into oblivion
Trapped somewhere between consciousness and
    irrelevance
The shadow too is welcome here
And it returns to replenish its spirit every once in a
    while

Lastly
Well lastly there's Grim
The love of my life
We've shared candlelit dinners
Walks in the park by moonlight
A glass of wine on the terrace
Grim never ceases to amaze me
Only problem is his best friend is my suitor

So what do I do
For now, I'll just answer the knocking on my door
Guess when Death loses its key, it can come knocking

When he dropped the paper onto the nightstand, Krystal shifted so she could look him in the eyes.

"I'm not going to lie to you. There've been times when I thought I couldn't handle things. I mean, coming here, cutting off my old friends and my parents has been hard. I think that's part of the reason I've kept in touch with my sister. I've had days when I just wanted to give up on everything." She turned around to face him. She wanted him to see in her eyes what he meant to her. "But then you show up. It's almost like you have a sixth sense. Whenever I needed you, somehow you were always there."

She turned back around, settling into his arms again before giving him the short answer to his question. The setting sun just outside of their window warmed her cheeks. She inhaled deeply, releasing the breath slowly, intentionally giving her mind a few seconds more to live in this moment because she knew what she was about to say would change both of their lives.

"The truth is," she began, "the first year, on the anniversary of Jerad's death, I thought about it." She felt Yohan tense behind her. She'd just stabbed him in the heart. She just hoped he'd be able to forgive her. "I even went as far as pulling the butcher's knife from the block in the kitchen and filling the tub with hot water. Then the phone rang, and it was you on the other line, telling me to come open the front door. I knew then that I couldn't do it. I loved you too much then to do it, and I haven't considered it since."

Yohan leaned down. Turning her to face him, his lips brushed across hers. Though the thought of her taking her life pained him, her answer gave him hope that he could continue to help her through any challenge she faced. He wanted to be there for her, show her real love, support her in any way that he could. He knew he couldn't take away her pain, but he was determined to help her experience life in the most joyous light possible.

Chapter Thirteen

Krystal settled into a routine with her new schedule. The last three weeks, most of her free time was tied up with therapy. At her therapist's suggestion, she'd even started a journal. Most times, writing helped her sort out her feelings. It kept her mind occupied so that she didn't dwell on the thoughts of Jerad.

But tonight was different. The longer Krystal wrote in her journal, the closer the walls seemed to get. She was suffocating in the house. She'd promised Yohan she'd be all right while he went to meet with The Trio, but if she stayed in this place any longer, she was sure she'd go crazy.

She picked up the cordless phone. Dialing China's number, her foot tapped as she waited for her to answer the phone.

"What's up, girl?" the voice on the other end bellowed.

Krystal listened as China's son screamed. "Not much. I guess you're kinda busy tonight."

"A little bit. Toi was supposed to be coming by to

spend some time with his son. We both know how that goes."

Krystal could only imagine the frown on China's face. She'd told her friend time and time again to leave that man alone. She agreed that Toi had every right to see his child, but one of them needed to clearly draw the line. She was more than sure that her friend was still attached to her child's father, but she needed to realize that he was married now and had another child at home.

"Yeah. Well, I was thinking about going out." Krystal stretched out across the bed, flipping through the hundreds of channels of nothing on the television.

"With who? Isn't Yohan working tonight?"

"Well," she hesitated, wondering if she really should be telling China about her new friend. Then she figured what the hell. "I met a new friend the other day."

"Friend? And where exactly did you meet this friend?"

"At the park." She rolled over on her side, tossing the remote on the nightstand. The night called to her, and she desired nothing more than to answer.

"Are you sure that's a good idea? I mean, if the guys found out—"

Krystal interrupted before China could complete her thought. "Right now, I don't much care about what the guys think. I need to get out of this house and soon." Before she knew it, she'd slid the glass door open and stepped out onto the balcony.

"What do you know about this guy?"

"His name is Octavio and he's here visiting some friends. And he's a cutie too." A bad feeling came over Krystal. The speech was coming, she was sure of it.

"Look, if you're going to do something stupid like see another man, at least be smart about it. Meet him in a public place."

"Na duh. I was thinking about going to Triple Threat."

Entering the house again, Krystal headed for the living room to grab her purse. She rambled through the numerous sets of keys, papers, and tubes of lip gloss until she located the folded paper with Octavio's number on it. She'd almost programmed it in her phone, but decided against it just in case.

"That would be public enough. It's a nice spot. I've been there a couple of times."

"Cool. Well, I'd better see if my 'friend' has any plans for tonight. I'll hit you up later and let you know how it goes." She twirled the paper between her fingers, a sudden rush of excitement filling her. Not only was she getting out of the house, she was finally going somewhere without the guys or Yohan scrutinizing her every move.

"Keep your phone on you and call me if you need anything."

"You know I will. Later."

The two ended their conversation and Krystal picked up her two-way pager. She sent a text message to her new friend, asking him to hit her up if he wasn't busy. Before she could put the pager down, he'd replied to her message. She picked up the phone and dialed the number he'd put in his message.

"What's up, sexy?" the male voice greeted on the other end of the line.

"Not much. Need to get out of the house." She cracked her neck before lying on her stomach on the bed. Her heels kicked in the air as she smiled from ear to ear. She still couldn't believe she was about to do this.

"I'm game. You want me to come get you?"

"Naw. You know where Triple Threat is?"

"The club?"

Krystal snickered at his question. There weren't too many places in the ATL named Triple Threat. "Yep."

"I think I can manage to find it."

"Meet me there in an hour." She jumped up from the bed, rushing out of the room, headed for her closet. She had so much to do and now the clock was ticking.

"Cool. See you there, sexy."

Krystal hung up the phone and stepped into the closet. Now she needed to decide what to wear. She wanted something a little provocative but not too sleazy. Rambling through the shelves of clothes, she pulled out a black leather skirt and a lilac silk halter top. Within twenty minutes, she was dressed, her hair up in a bouncy ponytail and her makeup done. Walking quickly to the bus stop at the entrance to the complex, Krystal climbed onto the bus headed for the club.

Krystal's two-way message surprised Octavio. He expected her to call, but not this soon, and he definitely hadn't expected her to ask him out. He'd planned to just sit back and relax. However, a little cutie had changed those plans. He looked forward to finding out what made her tick. And who knows? He might even get some work done while at it.

Octavio dressed quickly, wanting to get to the club and scope out the place before his date arrived. On the drive to the spot, he found his mind wondering why she'd decided to go out with him tonight instead of her usual posse.

Waiting in the parking lot, Octavio watched the young lady he'd met a few days earlier climb from the confines of the MARTA bus and step confidently onto the grassy sidewalk. He'd parked in the mini-mall parking lot a block or so away to wait for her. He assumed she was going to catch a ride with a friend or call a cab. Even though she wasn't his girl, he'd never have allowed her to make her own travel arrangements if he'd known she was going to ride the bus.

He watched as she pulled her cell phone from the small handbag held close to her chest. The low cut of the top drew his eyes downward. His tongue swiped over his lips as his vision followed the line of her cleavage to where the neckline disappeared beneath the tie of her jacket.

He shook the adult thoughts from his head in a mad attempt to regain his composure. He couldn't lose focus. This one was his ticket to early retirement, and he needed to keep that in mind. Besides, as far as he knew, she was a minor. If anything happened between them and it got out, he'd be screwed seven ways to Sunday. With all of the child molestation cases on the news in the past weeks, priests fondling altar boys, principals having affairs with students, not to mention stars accused of sleeping with underaged boys, Octavio wasn't even sure he should be here meeting Krystal this time of night. The ringing of his phone deflated the thoughts floating through his mind like hot air balloons.

"I see you," he replied in a voice not his own. It reminded him of the voices in the movies, where the man was stalking his female prey in an attempt to rattle her sense of security.

"Where are you?"

He watched her hair fling side to side as she searched for him. "Look behind you and follow the flashing lights."

Krystal turned, scanning the full parking lot behind her until she spotted the flickering headlights of the cherry red Dodge Durango.

He watched her step over the soft part of the fir-lined island separating the parking lot from the main street. The heels of her slide-on shoes flapped against her feet as she made her way across the lot.

Blood rushed from his brain to the unspoken place as

she approached. Images of his tongue running up and down her caramel body crept into his mind. The swelling between his legs pulsed with need. He needed to regain control, and fast.

Leaning over, he swung the passenger's door open for her. A rush of cool, moist air entered the vehicle, carrying with it the sweet smell of tangerine, chocolate, and lust. He reached out to her, disguising his need to touch her with a simple gesture to help her into the truck.

"I figured you'd be at the club waiting for me. I was just calling to let you know I'd be there in a minute." She adjusted her coat to cover her thighs.

"Lucky I decided to wait for you to call; saved you a little walk." His eyes roamed up her legs until they reached the belt of her coat. He continued his inspection until his gaze came to rest at her chest.

Krystal smirked, realizing he was looking everywhere but in her face. "True. I appreciate you meeting me out here. I was going crazy in the house."

"No problem." He gripped the steering wheel, closing his eyes to focus on one thing: control. Starting the engine, he pulled out of the parking space. "You should have let me come get you. I'd have never agreed to you riding the bus out here."

"Don't worry. I'm a big girl. I've been riding the bus late at night for years. It doesn't bother me. And neither do the people."

He glanced over to see the scowl on her face. "That's not a good look for you."

"So I've been told. But it keeps the creeps off of my back." She'd made her point. She could take care of herself. She just wished the guys would realize that as well.

"I can see why."

Pulling to a stop in front of the sign reading TRIPLE

THREAT, Octavio handed the valet the keys. He exited the vehicle and walked to the other side to help Krystal out. Walking right past the line formed in front of the door, Octavio handed the bouncer two crisp one-hundred-dollar bills. The man lifted the red velvet rope, allowing them passage into the club's domain.

Entering the doorway, Krystal felt the eyes of the bouncer burrowing into her. His brow furrowed, eyes narrowed as he tried to place where he knew her face. She slipped around the corner, out of his line of vision, as Octavio wrapped his hand around her wrist, nearly dragging her directly onto the crowded dance floor.

A moment more of contemplation and the bouncer remembered from where he knew the young lady. Grabbing his cell phone from the holster on his belt, he dialed the number to the club manager's office.

"What is it? I'm a little busy."

"A problem with a capital *P* just walked in our front door."

"So how is Krystal adjusting to therapy?" Aubrey asked, handing Yohan a glass of scotch. He and his brothers had allowed the couple some time to adjust, but in keeping with their promise to Jerad, Aubrey wanted to follow up to make sure Krystal was getting the help she needed.

"She's starting to open up. After the first couple of sessions, she and the doc have spent most of the time talking about us."

"Really?" His response surprised Aubrey. Not seeing how talking about her current relationship would help her deal with Jerad's death, Aubrey hoped the therapist knew what she was doing.

"Yeah. Don't ask me why." Yohan took a gulp from the

gold liquid sloshing around in his glass. He paid little attention to Aubrey walking across the room to once again stand in front of window.

Everyone in the office worked in his own little world. Andre sat perched in front of the security monitors, reviewing the bar tapes from the previous night. Antonio sat at the other desk counting stacks of ten- and twenty-dollar bills. Other than the few minutes it took him to make the two drinks, Aubrey had spent most of the night staring out of the window into the crowd below.

The four of them spent countless hours in the confines of this office. If the walls could speak, the feds would have a field day. Numbers running, sports betting, crooked real estate: you name it, The Trio had their hands in the pot. Aubrey was quite the gambler. Of course, the biggest gamble they took each night was tweaking the books to show just enough profit to not bring the IRS knocking on their doors.

For the first time since the club had opened, Yohan examined the office decor. A sea of white, black, and gold surrounded him on three of four sides. Behind him, hidden beneath a Clementine Hunter original painting, hung a fifty-inch plasma screen television they spent numerous nights perched in front of playing the latest Xbox games. The white leather couch he sat on blended in perfectly with the two black leather chairs, the white marble entertainment cabinet, and the white marble desk where Andre sat. The entertainment center and the chairs were trimmed in gold.

Yohan turned again to watch Aubrey stare into the main area of the club. He hadn't moved from the two-way mirror in twenty minutes. Yohan never understood the purpose of the mirror. The owner's office was nestled above the action in the main club area. It was hidden in the shadows of the rafters and the flashing lights that hung from the ceiling. The staircase leading to the office was hidden behind a drape, so unless you were looking for it, you'd never know it was there.

Standing, Yohan joined Aubrey in front of the window. "What's up?"

"I don't know." He shook his head. "I can't shake the feeling that something just isn't right."

"Not right how?" Yohan scanned the crowd, searching for anyone or anything out of place.

"I'm not sure what, I'm not sure when, but something's going to happen tonight."

Before Yohan could ask his next question, a knock on the door drew their attention. Antonio stashed the cash and grabbed his pistol as he eased over to the door. Peering through the peephole, he swung the door open. A short, pudgy man in a white suit and Hawaiian shirt stepped through the doorway. Antonio took one quick look at the club manager before making his way over to the couch and opening his cell phone.

"Aubrey, may I have a word with you?" the man asked.

Aubrey turned back to the window, again focusing on the crowd to look for the reason giving him the unsettling feeling. "What is it?"

"Can we speak in private?" The man shuffled his feet as he glanced around the room at Yohan and the other members of The Trio. He wiped his palms on his pants while grabbing the handkerchief from his pocket to dab the beads of sweat forming on his forehead.

Aubrey had never seen the manager this shaken. He was sweating profusely and the wringing of his hands was a bad sign. "After you." Aubrey allowed the man to precede him over the threshold. Once completely in the narrow walkway separating the back door from the metal stairwell, Aubrey pushed the door up enough to keep curious ears at bay.

"Now what's the problem?" Brey leaned his back against the wall, trying his best not to be intimidating. The little man was nervous enough without him towering over him like he naturally did.

Though The Trio never blamed him for the few problems they'd had at the club, having to inform them of a problem he couldn't handle always made him nervous. His position required him to deal with the problems in the day-to-day activities of Triple Threat, but this particular situation was beyond his scope of authority. Any issues concerning members of the LHC had strict orders to be handled directly by The Trio. The Krystal situation was definitely a Trio issue.

"There's a problem downstairs," he finally said, not looking his boss in the face.

"I kind of gathered that. What kind of a problem?"

Taking a deep, cleansing breath and slowly releasing it, hoping to control the quiver in his voice, the manager said the words, "Krystal's downstairs with some guy we don't know."

He waited for some reaction from Aubrey. All he got was a raised eyebrow and twist of the mouth.

"Thanks for letting me know. We'll take care of it." Aubrey opened the door and stepped back into the office, allowing the man to walk ahead of him and back out the front door. At least now he knew what the unsettling gut feeling he'd had all night was about.

Funny thing was he thought he'd seen Krystal not too long ago in the crowd. He'd dismissed the woman, though, sure his eyes were just playing tricks on him. Now he knew for sure the woman was Krystal.

Pushing the door closed, with the click of the lock engaging, Aubrey called out in a calm voice, "Yohan, finish up the security tapes. We have some business to tend to."

Andre and Antonio's stares followed Aubrey's path across the room, back to the window. The twins looked at each other with narrowed eyes, understanding the phrase, *business to tend to*. It usually meant trouble, LHC trouble.

Andre stood, his attention pulled away from the monitor, giving Yohan space to sit down and continue reviewing the tapes. Antonio ended his phone call and joined his brothers in front of the window. Aubrey scanned the crowd again, trying to locate the woman with the burgundy highlights and low-cut lilac halter top.

"There she is," he said under his breath just loud enough for his brothers to hear. Krystal was scantily clad and dancing a little too close to an older guy. Aubrey's anger escalated as he watched the man groping her.

"Who?" Dre asked.

"I'll explain on the way down."

Chapter Fourteen

No longer able to deny the hypnotic beat entering into her body, Krystal relaxed as the music took up residence. She allowed the rhythm to dictate her movements. Closing her eyes, she felt her body sway to the constant reggae beat. The feel of Octavio wrapping his fingers around her waist and pulling her close didn't faze her. The only thing that mattered was the beat pulsing through her veins, racing to and from every nerve in her body. It felt good to let go and live a little. She'd had so much on her mind for so long, she'd forgotten what it was like to just throw caution to the wind and live in the moment.

Descending the staircase, Aubrey revealed the problem to his brothers. "Krystal's down here with some dude."

"What the fuck!" Andre exclaimed.

Aubrey continued his descent, not taking time to acknowledge the surprise in his brother's voice. He only had one thing on his mind: getting Krystal away from that guy. When he reached the bottom stair, he turned to face his brothers. "We split up. I'll take care of the guy."

"I'll take Krystal," Andre proclaimed with a scowl that only he could see in the darkened walkway.

"I guess that leaves me to make sure no one runs."

"You got it." Aubrey turned his back to his brothers and swung the door open. Entering the club, they went their separate ways to take their positions. Aubrey watched Antonio circle around the dance floor. The reaction on his face indicated the exact moment he pinpointed Krystal.

Scanning the crowd on the other side, Aubrey spotted Andre in front of the bar. Dre stared at Krystal, watching the guy grind his groin into her behind. Aubrey took one last glance up at the office mirror knowing he couldn't see in, but hoping Yohan was still absorbed in the tapes. Then, he took his first steps toward the floor, seeing his brothers following suit.

The Trio slipped into stealth mode, weaving through the crowd. Krystal and her partner danced near the center of the floor oblivious to the impending danger creeping through the crowd around them. She had her eyes closed, so she never saw Andre approaching in front of her or Antonio to her right.

Octavio didn't pay any attention to the approaching men until he felt something solid being pressed into his back.

"Mind if we cut in?" Aubrey whispered directly into the man's ear. Though he had the pistol concealed and pointed at the man's back, Aubrey hoped he didn't have to use it.

Octavio froze as the barrel of the gun pushed firmer against his spine. It only took Krystal a moment to realize he'd stopped moving behind her. Opening her eyes, she stared into a not-so-happy pair of hazel eyes.

Trying her best not to panic, she inched her way away from Octavio. It was then she turned to her right to find Antonio standing there, feet shoulder width apart, arms crossed, gawking at her like a disappointed parent. With Andre in front of her and Antonio to her right, through the process of elimination, she assumed Aubrey was behind her, which meant he was behind Octavio.

Aubrey leaned over again to whisper into Octavio's ear, making sure the man still felt the barrel of the gun in his back. "Now, I'm going to lower my weapon and let you go. I want you to exit my establishment as quickly as your tiny legs will allow, or I'll have security personally escort you out. And trust me, you don't want security escorting you off of the premises. Understand?"

Octavio nodded his confirmation.

"We'll make sure this young lady—and I do stress *young*—makes it home safely. Now go."

Octavio relaxed as the barrel moved away from his spine. He inched his way from Aubrey's grasp. Taking one last glance at Krystal, he disappeared into the crowd.

Krystal was about to explain when Aubrey held up his hand to stop her. "Save it."

She rolled her eyes and sucked her teeth as he turned his back and walked away. She didn't care that he was upset. They'd never had a problem before with her doing what she wanted to do, so she didn't see what the problem was now.

She followed Aubrey and Antonio through the crowd with Andre close on her heels, and for the first time, she wondered what they were doing here. She'd chosen this club because China and some of her other classmates said it was a nice place and the music was great. It never occurred to her that this might be the club that The Trio owned, though maybe it should have, considering it was named Triple Threat.

Yohan's eyes lifted over the top of the monitor as the office door swung open. He watched as Aubrey entered with a scowl on his face. Right behind him, Antonio entered with just as much anger in his eyes. Then, as Antonio stepped to the side, he realized the source of the displeasure.

He watched as Krystal's eyes grew wide the minute she caught a glimpse of his face. Yohan narrowed his gaze, staring at her, not sure how to feel. Anger crept into his being, but soon disappointment overshadowed it. He tried to think rationally about the situation, even giving her the benefit of the doubt until he glanced down at the outfit she wore. Taking in the sight of the low-cut top and miniskirt, the only thought that ran through his mind was where in the hell were her clothes.

She stopped in the doorway, the confidence she'd only moments before held slipping from her body. She lowered her eyes, no longer able to hold Yohan's gaze. She didn't want to face the hurt in them. She never intended for him to find out about tonight.

"What you stopping fo'?" The voice behind her said, "You was all big and bad dancing like a hoochie downstairs. Don't be acting all scared now." Andre nudged her into the office and slammed the door behind him. He leaned his back against it and crossed his arms. His smirk said it all. He wanted to hear what kind of explanation she was going to give now that she had to face her man.

"Have a seat," Aubrey instructed.

Krystal shied away from her boyfriend's unwavering eyes, taking care to cross her legs when she sat down on the leather couch.

"Now, care to enlighten us as to what you called yourself doing downstairs?"

"Fuck that!" Yohan interrupted. "I wanna know where the hell are your clothes?"

Krystal's attempt to pull the coat closed over her knees failed; the opening revealing the lack of covering for her thick thighs. She fidgeted, uncomfortable with the way Yohan was eyeballing her. Finally she stood, no longer able to contend with his scrutiny. She didn't respond to any of them. Instead her eyes focused on the ground, trying her best to avoid their judgmental stares.

"Well, young lady?" Antonio said. "We're waiting. Is there anything you want to say for yourself?"

"Not much I can say," she replied in a timid voice, still unable to bring her eyes away from the floor to look at any of them.

Yohan stood, his movements forcing his chair to slide across the floor and abruptly stop as it slammed into the wall. He glanced around the room at The Trio. Their eyes remained fixated on Krystal. They wanted answers and so did he, but he knew they wouldn't get them by ganging up on her.

"Get your purse and let's go," he said through gritted teeth, trying his best to keep his anger under control. He made his way to the door as Andre stepped aside. Opening it, Yohan glared at Krystal as she inched her way past him out of the room. He looked back at all of them one last time before closing the door behind them.

"There's going to be hell to pay when they get home." Antonio could only imagine what it would be like to be a fly on the wall during that conversation.

"There needs to be. Krystal was wrong and she knows it. It's not the fact that she came down here dressed like a prostitute that concerns me, though. I'm wondering how she got down here, and most of all who the guy was," Aubrey replied with a not-so-happy tone.

"I was thinking that same thing. Even if she caught a ride, that guy was a little old to be in this crowd. I wonder—" Before Andre could finish his thought, the office phone rang. He snatched it from the cradle, knowing it had to be the manager on the other line. "Yeah?"

"Hey. I've got someone here who has something to tell you."

"Can't this wait?" Andre made sure the club manager understood that this was not the time to interrupt them.

"He says it has to do with the guy Krystal was with."

Andre raised an eyebrow. "Who is it?"

"The new kid, Nigel."

"Put him on." Andre pressed the button to activate the speakerphone so they could all hear what Nigel had to say. "We're listening."

"Yo, that dude Krystal was with tonight, I seen him before." Nigel knew following that guy would pay off. He'd been seeing him around Lincoln Heights a lot lately and he got a bad vibe from the guy.

"Where?" Andre asked.

"In Lincoln Heights. A couple of weeks ago when Krystal was out of school. I went by the park and she was out there talking to that dude. He got into a red Dodge Durango with Virginia plates."

"Anything else, little birdie?"

"Naw. I didn't think nothing of it until I saw her come in with him tonight."

"We'll take it from here." Andre severed the connection.

"I don't like this." Aubrey and Andre turned at the sound of their brother's voice.

"What's up, baby bro?" Andre asked his twin. In his head, he could feel that Tonio was disturbed. True, the information Nigel had just provided was troubling, but he felt there was something more to his brother's concern.

"I got a bad feeling about this. I need to talk to Yohan."

Aubrey gave his brother a curious glance. He knew how close Antonio and Yohan were, and much of Yohan's past he only shared with Antonio. Aubrey wondered if something Nigel said had anything to do with Yohan's life prior to Lincoln Heights. Before he got the chance to ask, Antonio was up and out of the back door.

"What do you think that was about?" Aubrey asked.

"I don't know, but I get the feeling there's more to this than we know."

Yohan didn't know what to say to Krystal, so he chose not to say anything at all. So many thoughts raced through his mind. He wondered how she'd gotten to the club, how long she'd been there, as well as who she was there with. Not to mention, he was still concerned about the way she was dressed. He knew she had some provocative clothes— they shared a closet—but he didn't recall her ever wearing anything as revealing as what she had on.

He struggled with the words hankering to escape his mouth. One minute he wanted to just reach over and shake some sense into her, the next he wanted to yell at her like she was a child and even still, a moment later, he wanted to just pull her into his arms and hold her.

He snuck glimpses of her from the corner of his eye as he drove. Her rambling was working his last nerve. She kept saying the same things over and over. He only listened to bits and pieces of what she said: something about being sorry and not meaning to disappoint him. She went on and on about how she was bored in the house and how the walls felt like they were closing in and how she had to do something but she wanted for a change to do something on her own.

He didn't say a word to her the entire trip home. Instead, he just listened to her babbling as she tried to convince him and herself that she'd done nothing wrong. Pulling into the parking spot, he could only think of how naive she sounded. They had good reason to make sure she always had an escort. There were people out there who'd do anything to get at The Trio, including using her.

"Are you even listening to me?"

Again, Yohan didn't respond. He tightened his grip on

the steering wheel, fighting the growing urge to reach over and slap her.

"Oh, so now you gon' give me the silent treatment," she huffed, rolling her eyes, waiting for him to say something.

After a moment more of sulking and pouting like a two-year-old, Krystal swung the door open and climbed out of the truck. Slamming the door, she stomped away, sure by the time she reached the stairwell he'd be turning the ignition off and following.

To her surprise, he spun the tires, backing out of the space. Revving the engine, he whipped around the corner of the building, narrowly missing a group of guys about to cross the street and a red Dodge Durango. All Krystal could do was stare at his taillights as they disappeared out of sight. He'd come back after he cooled off. At least she hoped so.

For the fifth time, Yohan glowered at the ringing cell phone in the passenger seat. He ignored the first four times it rang, but the racket was getting on his last nerve. Talking to Krystal at the moment was definitely not a good idea. Grabbing the phone, he flung it toward the back, flinching at the sound of it crashing against the vinyl middle console.

He drove around for hours, blaming himself for her showing up at the club tonight. Apparently, he'd been neglecting her again, and he needed to figure out how to rectify the situation. He'd failed her and the notion was eating away at his confidence. He was supposed to protect her no matter what. He'd promised The Trio he was committed to the challenge, but now he was beginning to doubt his ability to provide Krystal with the protection she needed and deserved.

What she'd done tonight was dangerous on so many levels. She needed to know that. Only problem, how to tell her without frightening her or revealing too much information? She'd have questions, many of which he wouldn't be able to answer, so responding to this situation called for more than tact. And he had another concern. Though they hadn't said anything, he was sure The Trio was going to question whether he was capable of the level of protection Krystal required.

After three hours of riding around the city, with more unanswered questions now than he'd had when he left, Yohan pulled into his parking spot in front of his apartment. The bedroom lights were out, so he assumed Krystal was asleep. Searching the back of the truck, he located the pieces of the cell phone and put it back together. Climbing the stairs leading to his apartment, he listened to the voice mail messages.

One by one, he pressed delete as Krystal's voice changed from anger to sadness and eventually to worry. By the time he got to the last message, he could hear how sorry she was. Assuming the last message was also from her, he almost deleted it without listening, but before his finger hit the delete button he heard Antonio's voice.

The short message instructed him to call as soon as he got the message. Something didn't sound right. Antonio sounded concerned. Yohan quickly dialed Tonio's cell number.

"Where are you?" Antonio wasted no time with formalities.

"About to walk into the house."

"Come downstairs. I need to talk to you."

"Be there in a minute." Yohan ended the call and quickly made his way back down the stairs.

Antonio stood at the door waiting for him.

"What did you need to talk about?" Yohan asked as he sat down on the couch.

"Have you noticed any unusual activities while doing

your rounds?" Antonio leaned against the wall, his attention placed squarely on Yohan. If this guy had been in Lincoln Heights, Yohan should have noticed.

Yohan thought for a moment, trying to remember if he'd seen any strange faces or new vehicles. He didn't recall anything or anyone new since he'd run across Nigel.

"Not that I can think of. Why?"

"We received some disturbing information tonight. The guy in the club with Krystal. Ya boy Nigel said he's seen him around Lincoln Heights. He said the guy drives a red Durango with Virginia plates."

"You don't think . . ." For the first time, Yohan started to put the pieces together: the red SUV at Krystal's school, the one by the building when he left to do his rounds. It was even there when he'd left her standing in front of their apartment earlier tonight. How could he have been so stupid?

"I don't know. Do you think they're looking for you?" Antonio had tried to warn him that he needed to tie up the loose ends of his past, but Yohan refused to go back.

"I can't imagine why. The police ruled her death an accident." Yohan stood, walking from one side of the room to the other. He balled his fist, trying to block out the memories of a night he wanted to forget.

"And her parents?"

"It's always possible, I guess. I'm pretty sure they're still blaming me for the accident." He pinched the bridge of his nose. His head was starting to hurt.

"I just wanted to let you know to keep an eye out. Let me know if you see this guy." This was too close to home for Yohan. Antonio wasn't sure he'd be able to handle this without it getting messy.

"I can handle it," Yohan replied at the implication that he was slipping on the job. He turned, making his way to the door.

"And what about Krystal? You still okay as far as she's concerned?"

Yohan whipped around to stare Antonio in the face. "I can handle my responsibilities, and Krystal is my responsibility." He stormed out the door, slamming it closed behind him.

Chapter Fifteen

Adjusting the seat to an upright position, Yohan stretched. He looked out to the field and smiled as Krystal completed two backflips and a handspring before finishing the combination with a split. The other girls were packing up the banner for next week's basketball game while China grabbed the rest of Krystal's things.

The digital clock in the truck read 6:45 and the sky was beginning to cloud over. Yohan had decided to come early just to keep an eye on her. Since the night at the club, things between them had been strained. It wasn't that he didn't trust her, but The Trio was being tight-lipped about the details of that night, and he still had the nagging feeling that they were keeping something from him.

He watched the football players grab their gear and head up the stairs toward the gym. As he turned again in Krystal's direction, he noticed a brown-skinned older-looking guy dressed in black leaning against the fence, watching the cheerleaders gather their belongings. He watched as the man walked around the side of the fence where the gate, now half hanging from the pole, swung in the light breeze. His concern grew, and before he knew it, he was out of the truck making his way toward where Krystal and China stood.

"What's up, sexy?" Octavio asked, approaching Krystal from behind.

She turned around, startled at the sound of his voice. She'd been so absorbed in her conversation with China she hadn't noticed him approaching.

"What are you doing here?" She looked up toward the parking lot, attempting to locate Yohan. She knew he was there; she'd seen his truck drive by earlier. She expected at any moment he'd be upon them. "It's not safe for you to be here."

"Don't worry your pretty little head. I just hadn't heard from you in a couple of days and I wanted to make sure you were all right. Just hit me up a little later." He flashed her a sincere smile then turned and walked in the other direction. As he passed the tennis courts, he saw her boyfriend approaching.

Yohan stopped in the middle of the staircase watching as the strange man who'd just spoken to Krystal approached. The man continued his stride, not looking in his direction or saying so much as one word.

After only a moment of hesitation, Yohan turned, prepared to pursue the man now at the top of the staircase, but the guy climbed into a red SUV and pulled off. Unfortunately, he didn't catch the license plate number.

"What's up?" Krystal asked, stopping one step below Yohan.

His head snapped around at the sound of her voice. "Who was that?" He raised an eyebrow, crossing his arms and looking down at her.

Not sure if it was anger, concern, or jealousy she detected, Krystal replied drily, "Nobody. Now let's go home." She continued up the staircase, not saying another word about Octavio.

Yohan's eyes followed her ascent and for the first time, he questioned her fidelity. Her short answer troubled him. It wasn't like her to be elusive. The longer he watched her, the greater the sense of uneasiness became. He searched his memory, attempting to determine if he'd ever seen the guy before. Damn. He wished he'd paid more attention to the license plate. The man's face looked vaguely familiar, but with the baseball cap pulled over his eyes, Yohan didn't get a good look.

"Are you coming?" Krystal yelled to him from the top of the stairs. Her foot bounced on the pavement as she glowered at him.

Choosing to ignore her attitude, Yohan climbed the stairs and helped her into the truck. Sliding into the driver's seat and pulling out of the parking lot, he asked, "You feel like going out tonight?"

She gave his question some thought. It had been a while since they'd done anything on a Friday night. She usually had a game or a cheerleading competition and the few weekends she'd had off, Yohan had to work. This was their off week, and if he wanted to spend some time together, she was more than willing to oblige.

"What exactly did you have in mind?"

"It's a surprise." He couldn't hide his smile.

"Isn't everything with you a surprise?" She crossed her arms and gawked at him.

Yohan chose his smirk as his only form of acknowledgment to her comment. They'd have a good time tonight. He'd make sure of it.

Yohan rolled to a stop in front of the sign reading DAVE AND BUSTER'S. Climbing from the driver's side, Yohan handed the valet his keys and grabbed the ticket the man held out to him. He opened an umbrella, shielding his head from the light drizzle. Though the night had arrived hours earlier, the many lights in the parking lot and around the entrance to the building lit a path as far as the eye could see.

Making his way around the rear of the vehicle, a girl, no more than fifteen, stopped him.

"What's up, shawdy? Can I get a ride?"

He gave her the once-over before responding, "Sorry, I don't do jailbait." Then he proceeded to grab their pool cues and help Krystal from the truck.

Once inside, Krystal and Yohan climbed up the four stairs and turning to the left, Krystal scooted her way through the line of people at the reservations desk while Yohan added their names to the list for a pool table. Her back against the wall, she looked over the railing at the crowd forming below. The sound of a woman's scream coming from the main restaurant area grabbed her attention. With nowhere to go, she pressed as much as possible into the wall as the crowd advanced in her direction.

Suddenly, a teenaged boy in a white T-shirt covered in what looked like blood forced his way through the crowd, running furiously in her direction. The next thing she knew, someone grabbed her around the waist and pulled her in the opposite direction. The young man leapt in what seemed like a frame-by-frame action, over the balcony into the crowd below, eventually making it out of the door.

"He didn't hit you, did he?" Yohan asked, not sure he'd gotten her out of the way in time. He scooted into the narrow space between the reservations desk and the office door reading EMPLOYEES ONLY.

"No," she replied, rubbing her arms to ward off a shudder.

Yohan pulled her closer, and they scooted toward the corner to get out of the way of the fast-moving crowd. The couple watched as two plainclothes and three uniformed officers escorted a fairly large, bloodied male to the stairs and out of the door. The air buzzed with voices, many of which stated that they'd seen what happened and how the fight broke out.

The commotion quickly died down and Yohan kept a close watch on Krystal, still not confident that she was really all right. Within twenty minutes, they were out of the game room and Krystal was practicing her shots at their table.

"I'm going to the bar. You gonna be all right while I'm gone?"

Krystal placed the nine ball in its slot among the others and centered the balls over the white dot on the table. Sliding the cue ball from Yohan's hand and giving him a seductive look, she replied, "Hurry back. Mama wants to play."

He leaned in to her, pinning her between his body and the pool table, her curves molding perfectly to his body. Leaning her over, helping her take aim, he whispered in her ear, "Be careful what you wish for. You know daddy's only here to please." Taking a quick nibble on her earlobe, Yohan left her and made his way to the bar.

He claimed a bar stool and waited for the bartender to finish with the other customers.

"What can I get you?"

"A rusty nail."

"Coming right up."

As the bartender stepped away to fill his drink order, Yohan turned in the direction of Krystal and their table.

"What's up, shawdy? Can a brotha play with you?"

Krystal cut her eyes at the young boy addressing her

as *shawdy*. She so hated that word. Sizing him up, his two sizes too big jersey and his pants hanging down nearly to his ankles, she decided to ignore him, hoping he and his friend would get the hint that she wasn't interested.

"Aye ho, I'm talking to you."

The guy stepped a little closer and immediately the smell of alcohol emanating from him caused her nose to burn. Her face twisted at the stench and she stepped back to put some distance between them.

"I asked you a question."

Continuing to ignore him, Krystal made her way to the other side of the table.

"Oh, I know this bitch didn't just brush me off," he said to his friend. The guy quickly walked to the other side of the table where Krystal stood. Just as he reached for her, Yohan caught his arm.

The youngster's eyes followed the line of the dark, muscular arm to the massive shoulder it was attached to. Eventually, he stared into a pair of angry, dark eyes.

Over the guy's shoulder, Yohan watched as his friend backed out of the way. "What did you just call my woman?"

"Aye, man. Get the fuck up off of me." The boy struggled to get out of Yohan's grip, but nearly twice his size and with the extra adrenaline pumping through his system, this little boy was in big trouble.

"And I know you was not just about to lay your hands on my woman."

Krystal witnessed the rage burning beneath Yohan's eyes. She also witnessed the fear beginning to fill the youngster's body language and expressions.

"Yohan, baby, let him go." Other than a quick glance, he ignored her request. "Yohan, think about what you're about to do. I don't have a license and the guys are at work. How am I supposed to get home if you get locked up?" She only paused to give him time to process what she'd just said. "Think about what happened when we first got here. Is it really worth it?"

Yohan twisted the boy's arm behind his back. "Apologize," he said, raising the boy's arm just enough to cause discomfort.

"I'm sorry."

"You're sorry what?" With a little additional "encouragement" the boy continued.

"I'm sorry for calling you out of your name."

The youngster was trying to hide his embarrassment and keep his composure, but Yohan continued to pull on his arm and there was no way for him to hide the pain.

"I'm going to let you go, but don't you ever again in life touch a woman if she doesn't want to be touched. You understand me?"

"Yes," the boy replied with his head held low.

"Yes what?"

"Yes, sir."

Pushing the youngster away, they watched the guy and his friend scurry through the crowd and out the door.

"Krystal?" Now that that was settled, Yohan turned his full attention back to his woman.

"I'm fine." She slid her arms around his waist, resting her head on his chest. "It's been quite an eventful night."

"You sound like you're ready to go home." He pulled away to look her in the face.

"I sure am, big daddy." She gave him a devilish grin. Grabbing her jacket and cues, she sashayed her way to the reservation desk.

Yohan downed his drink, collected his cues, and followed her. He knew what she had in mind, and he'd make sure she got exactly what she wanted.

Chapter Sixteen

A lack of oxygen snatched Krystal from her trouble-some slumber. She'd already had a long night and it seemed that it still wasn't over. Holding her chest as she gasped for air, she felt more tears rush from her eyes. Sitting up, she focused on her breathing, desperately trying to catch her breath.

"Krystal, you all right?" Yohan asked as he flipped the lamp on.

Panting, she replied, "Give me the phone."

He gave her an unsure look. It was nearly three in the morning. "What's wrong?"

"Don't ask me questions. Just give me the damn phone!"

Handing her the cordless phone from the cradle on the nightstand, he watched as she climbed out of the bed. As she dialed the number, her pacing in the narrow space between the bed and the wall created a whishing sound that echoed through their bedroom.

"Please be there. God, please be there," she repeated as she anxiously awaited an answer on the other end of the line.

"Krystal, what's wrong?" Yohan asked in one last attempt to get a response from her.

She cut her eyes at him, giving him a deathly stare.

"Fine. Forget I asked." He slid from beneath the covers and walked out of the bedroom.

"Hello," the groggy voice from the other end of the receiver said.

"China!"

"Huh?"

"China, wake up. Is Toi over there?"

"What? No. He went home to his wife."

"China! China, listen to me!"

"What, Krystal? It's three in the freaking morning."

"China, I had a dream."

China's eyes flew open and the pounding of her heart escalated to a nearly frantic pace. She was one of the few people who knew the truth behind Krystal's dreams. Taking a few deep breaths to calm her nerves, she asked, "What did you dream, Krystal?"

"I'll tell you in a minute. First we need to find Toi."

"Hold on." China clicked over to the other line. Within seconds, Krystal heard the line ringing.

"Hello?" a male voice responded.

China knew she was about to get cursed out, but that was the least of her worries. "Mason?"

"China, what do you want?"

"Mason, I need you to call your brother and make sure he's home." She waited for his anger. Instead, his reply remained calm.

"I'm not calling his house at three in the morning."

"Look, it's a matter of life and death."

"Is Hassan okay?" Mason leaned up in bed, concerned that something was wrong with his nephew.

"Yeah. Just call and make sure your brother's home, then call me back." China severed the connection with

Mason. He asked too many questions. If she wanted him to call his brother, she needed to get him off of the phone.

"Is he going to call?" Krystal asked.

"Oh, he'll call. Now you wanna tell me about this dream of yours?"

Her friend hadn't reached upset yet, but after what she had to tell her, that was destined to change. "You're not going to like it."

"I know, but I have to know."

"It didn't last long and strangely, it was in color. I remember his car hitting a metal trash can, and a newspaper clipping. I couldn't make out the headlines but there were two pictures. On one side was a picture of his car smashed up against some dark object. I can't remember if it was a building or a tree or what. On the other side, there's a picture of Toi."

"Anything else?" China's eyes watered as her heart sank.

"Yeah." Krystal took in a breath before continuing. "The date. The date on the paper is tomorrow's date. China, we have to find him. We gotta warn him." Her voice escalated along with her concern.

Before China got the chance to respond to Krystal's pleas, her line rang. "Hold on."

Krystal waited anxiously for China to click back over. She prayed Toi was at home with his wife; however, her gut was telling her otherwise. Her dreams never lied. The one she'd had about Jerad turned out to be right. So did the few she'd had of some of her classmates. Toi wasn't going to make it through another day, and there was nothing any of them would be able to do about it.

"Krystal?" China said with a tremble in her voice.

"He's not there, is he?"

China tried to say the word but found she couldn't. Krystal's dreams were never wrong. She'd been able to prevent the final outcome before. The only chance they had, though, required them to find the person and warn him. Knowing Toi the way she knew Toi, Krystal knew that was going to be nearly impossible.

"I'm so sorry, China. Look, just keep calling him and tell Mason to keep calling. Blow up his cell phone and pager if you have to. Just keep trying."

"He's going to die, isn't he?"

Krystal heard the fear in China's voice. She knew her friend was on the verge of tears and no amount of comfort would make things better. "I don't know. I just don't know. Look, call Mason back, tell him to keep trying to find his brother."

"And what am I supposed to tell him?" China was yelling now. "Am I just supposed to tell him my nutcase friend who dreams people's deaths saw a newspaper clipping with his brother on it and his car wrecked?"

Krystal remained calm. She understood what China was going through. She'd reacted the same way the first time she'd realized her dreams foretold others' deaths.

"China, listen to me. You can't give up. You have to believe you can find him. If you can warn him, all of this goes away. You understand?"

Between sniffles she replied, "Yes."

"Now call Mason back and call me later. Good luck, China. I really mean it. I'll be praying you find him."

"Thanks." China hung up the phone, leaving Krystal holding on to the other end listening to the dial tone.

Krystal knelt down on the floor next to the bed and cried. She cried for Toi because tonight he'd die. She cried for China because her friend was destined to raise their son on her own. She cried for Toi's son, Hassan, who'd grow up never knowing his father. But most of all, Krystal cried for herself. She was the bearer of bad news. She was the one who'd have to live with knowing Toi was going to be snatched from the lives of so many people and there was nothing she could do to prevent it.

Yohan crept back into the room at the sound of Krystal crying. He'd been angry with her when he'd walked out, sure she was hiding something from him. Now, seeing her on the floor weeping like a child, he knew whatever was bothering her was more than she could handle right now. He didn't know what it was, but she needed him. His anger dissipated as he lifted her from the floor and pulled her into his arms.

Krystal clung to him, sure if she let him go he'd leave her too. He'd promised to always be there for her, but Toi had made the same promise to China and where had it left her? With a child by a man who turned around and married another woman six months after their son was born.

Things were already hard enough. Toi dropped in and out of China and Hassan's lives on a whim. True, he made sure his son had the essentials, but all he'd ever done to China was string her along. Still, Krystal felt it unfair for China to have to do this alone. Hassan needed two parents. But after tonight, he'd only have one.

Yohan held her tighter as he felt her legs give way. Scooping her into his arms, he laid her on the bed. Sliding under the covers with her, he held on to Krystal as she rocked and cried herself to sleep.

After ten phone calls and no returned messages, Krystal gave up on reaching China. She'd even resorted to calling Mason. No one had heard a word from China or Toi. Finally, exhausted from the stress of worrying, Krystal decided to just let things be. She didn't have it in her to worry anymore. Sooner or later she'd get the call. Either Toi was alive or dead.

"Krystal?" The sound of Yohan's voice caught her off guard.

"Yeah?"

He sat on the bed next to her. She'd been sitting in their bedroom staring out of the window with the phone in her hand most of the morning. "Feel like getting out of the house for a little while?"

"I really should stay here just in case . . ." Her voice trailed off as thoughts of her dream flooded her mind. She turned from him. She hadn't told him about the dreams. He didn't need to know about her little curse.

"Come on. You've been cooped up in this room moping since you got up. Some air will do you good. Besides, anyone who can reach you here can reach you on your two-way, right?" Lifting her chin, he brushed away the tears running down her cheeks.

"I guess so."

"I won't keep you out long. I promise. Now get dressed." Yohan gave her a reassuring hug, and then he left her to get dressed.

Krystal glanced over at the clock on the radio, not realizing they'd been out over five hours. All had been quiet. No phone calls, no text message, nothing. She and Yohan spent most of the day in and out of record stores, wheel shops, and warehouse clubs. Someone was hosting a private party tonight at the club and he had the task of picking up the supplies in addition to his regular merchandise run.

Krystal stared out of the window, her attention drawn to the red Dodge in the side mirror. The dark tint of the windows prevented her from seeing the driver. She almost panicked, thinking Octavio was following them, but the SUV turned at the light as they continued through it.

Yohan drove and answered his ringing cell phone. The call was brief and by the time he hung up, he'd pulled into a gas station and turned around.

"Where are you going?"

He didn't respond. He didn't even take his eyes off of the road.

"Yohan, where are we going?"

Sadly, he replied, "I think China needs you."

Krystal lowered her head. "They found Toi, didn't they?"

Toi was a member of the LHC. She knew if they found him, The Trio would be the first to know and of course they'd call Yohan to tell her.

"Can I ask you something?" A gut feeling told him Krystal had some link to this. He just wished he knew what it was.

"What?" Silently, Krystal prayed he wasn't going to ask her what she thought he was going to ask.

"You knew, didn't you? You knew they'd find him dead. That's why you were upset last night."

"I can't talk about this right now."

"Why not?" His voice rose, though he hadn't meant for it to. "You can't keep this inside. I thought we decided we were going to talk about what's going on; that you weren't going to hide things from me anymore."

"What do you want me to say!" That was it. Krystal lost every bit of control she had. The words just poured out of her "I can't explain it. I just see it sometimes. I don't know why, I just do."

Her head flopped against the headrest as numbness invaded her body. She knew they'd find him. His fate had already revealed itself to her. Still, she didn't know how to react. She was angry and upset and deadened all at the same time. She expected the tears to begin any minute, but they didn't. She just stared out through the windshield as they made their way back to Lincoln Heights.

Chapter Seventeen

Toi's funeral was held in a small funeral home about ten miles from Lincoln Heights. The day was fitting for a funeral. The sky was overcast and a light mist hung in the air around them. The weather definitely fit the mood of everyone there to say their final good-byes to a friend.

Toi's mother gave China dirty looks most of the ceremony. It took both Krystal and Antonio to keep Yohan from going up to the woman and speaking his mind. China had every right to be there. Whether his mother liked it or not, Hassan was Toi's firstborn and though he was too young to remember any of this, he needed to see his father for the last time.

Once at the cemetery, Krystal and Yohan remained in the truck while Antonio accompanied China to the burial site. It was customary for one or all of the members of The Trio to make an appearance when someone from the LHC died. Today, though, only Antonio had shown up to pay his last respects. Aubrey was out of town and Andre had been nowhere to be seen for the last three days.

Antonio stood by China's side as Toi's family approached. He held Hassan in his arms, allowing China the freedom to mourn as she saw fit without worrying about his safety. Mason approached them first.

"Sorry about your brother," Antonio said, genuinely meaning the words. Outside of his cheating, Toi was a good man.

"Yeah, well, looks like his running around finally caught up with him." He turned to China. She looked sickly, like she hadn't eaten or slept in a couple of days.

"How you holding up?" he asked, placing a hand on her shoulder.

"Okay, I guess." She watched her son squirm in Antonio's arms, trying to get to his uncle.

"Mind if I hold him?"

"Go ahead. No matter what your mother thinks, Hassan's still your flesh and blood."

Mason lifted Hassan from Antonio's arms and hugged him securely. Hassan grabbed at his uncle's nose and ears as he tried his best to climb over Mason's shoulders. He giggled as Mason made faces at him and tickled his belly.

China lifted teary eyes to Antonio. She watched as he narrowed his and crossed his arms over his chest. He looked as if he was ready to start a fight.

"What's up, Antonio?" Mason asked, noticing the change in demeanor.

"Here comes your mother." Mason had his back to the grave, so he hadn't seen his mother approaching. "I'm telling you now, if she says the wrong thing I can't be held responsible for my actions. I ignored her sneers at China during the ceremony, but I will not allow your mother to upset her now. And she had better be glad Krystal was here because Yohan was about to give her a piece of his mind during the services."

"Krystal's here?" Mason scanned the crowd for them. He secretly had a crush on Krystal, but he'd never approached her because Yohan was forever by her side.

"She and Yohan are in the truck. She's dealing with a lot of issues right now. She only came to the funeral to support China."

Mason handed Hassan back to China as his mother stepped up beside him. He whispered something to her before excusing himself.

Ms. Martin regarded China with disdain. "You're one of the Fedichi boys, aren't you?" she asked the light-complexioned man standing at her son's baby mama's side.

"Yes, ma'am. I came to deliver my condolences on behalf of myself and my brothers." His expression relaxed at her civility.

"Well, thank you, young man." She then turned her attention back to China. In the politest voice she could muster, she asked, "May I hold my grandson?"

China looked over at Antonio for reassurance. He nodded his agreement and she slowly relinquished her son to his grandmother. The minute Hassan was completely in Ms. Martin's arms, he began kicking and screaming. He cried hysterically as he tried to get away from her. Hassan searched, his eyes darting back and forth for someone other than the woman holding him in her arms. The minute he laid eyes on Antonio, he reached out to him, fighting with what little strength he possessed, trying to get away from this woman he didn't know.

Antonio answered the little boy's pleas, taking Hassan from the woman. His tears stopped and as the sniffling receded, he again became the happy, giggly little boy he'd been with Mason. Ms. Martin gave China an evil look as if she'd had something to do with Hassan's temper tantrum.

"Don't look at her like that. She didn't have anything to do with Hassan's reaction to you." Ms. Martin had just crossed the line with her sneer. Antonio refused to hold his tongue any longer. "You're the one to blame for that. Hassan doesn't know you, and you only have yourself to blame. Come on, China, let's get you and Hassan home."

He grabbed her by the hand and they walked away, leaving Ms. Martin standing alone in the cemetery.

"A penny for your thoughts?" Yohan asked.

"It still doesn't feel real. I feel responsible for him, like it's partially my fault. I keep thinking if I'd tried to call one more time he'd still be alive." She twirled a lock of her hair, keeping her hands busy, distracting her mind. The shaking had stopped at the service, but the energy remained, so twirling her hair would just have to do.

"Don't blame yourself. If he'd been home with his family instead of running the streets, he'd still be alive."

"I know, but I can't get the thoughts out of my head." She sunk further into the seat, her heart weighted with sorrow. All she wanted to do was walk away from this.

"Who's that holding Hassan?"

Krystal narrowed her eyes, trying to see if she recognized the face of the man with the chubby, high yellow baby in his arms. "Mason. He's Toi's younger brother."

"I didn't know Toi had a brother," Yohan questioned.

"He doesn't live in Lincoln Heights."

"Oh."

Krystal observed the exchange between Antonio, China, and Mason. Hassan seemed right at home in his uncle's arms. Although he didn't come around much, Mason had formed a solid bond with his nephew the few times they had seen each other. Krystal hoped their exchange was a sign that, although Toi was dead, Mason would continue to be a part of his nephew's life. He deserved to know his father's family.

"Look," Krystal said to Yohan.

His face turned to a scowl. "That's Toi's mother, isn't it?"

"Yep. This should be interesting."

Their eyes remained fixated as the drama unfolded. Yohan found it strange that Mason walked away after his mother approached. It was no secret Toi's mother didn't like China and she took every opportunity to make her feelings known.

Yohan studied the woman's face as she attempted to smile and play nice to China. The expression was as fake as the woman the face belonged to. China amazed Yohan when she handed Hassan to the woman who'd only had negative words to say about her. He understood. She didn't want her son to suffer just because Ms. Martin didn't like her.

Just as Krystal expected, Hassan had a fit once he was in Ms. Martin's arms. It only lasted a moment. Antonio quickly took the distraught child from the clutches of the woman he seemed so afraid of. He said something to the woman, then grabbed China's hand, and they began walking back to the truck.

"Why'd he react that way?" Yohan asked in confusion.

"My grandmama used to always tell me babies could sense evil. They're so innocent that being around evil just does something to them. And that woman right there is full of it."

Krystal didn't say another word as Antonio strapped Hassan into the car seat, helped China into the truck, and slid in beside her. She turned around to see her best friend staring down at the life she and Toi had created. He was so precious, so innocent, and he deserved so much.

Antonio reached over and held China's hands. She turned from her son to look into his eyes.

"Don't worry. Hassan will have a father figure. We can't replace Toi, but my brothers and I will make sure he understands what it means to be a man."

During the ride home, no one said a word. Each person allowed him or herself to slip into a state of contemplation of the day's events. Strangely, the silence was comforting.

Chapter Eighteen

Krystal's life crept back into a state of normalcy. She smiled as the afternoon sun warmed her cheeks. Yohan had come and picked her up early from school so she could go with him to pick her sister up from the airport. Krystal didn't talk about her family much and whenever he broached the subject, she shifted the conversation in another direction.

He knew she still talked with her only sister, though. Sometimes he'd watch her for hours when she was on the phone with Myisha, her expressions remaining soft and joyful until Myisha mentioned their parents. The dreaded *parent* word changed Krystal's demeanor. Though Myisha couldn't see the expression, Krystal gave her sister the same expression she gave him whenever he mentioned her parents.

"If I didn't know any better, I'd swear you were excited about your sister's visit." Yohan kept his eyes on the road, taking extra caution as he bobbed through the traffic on I-285.

"I am and I can't wait to see my nephew," she replied, bubbling with excitement.

"What's with you and babies?"

"What are you talking about?" Krystal looked at him curiously, wondering what he was thinking.

"You sure have been spending a lot of time with the kids lately. And now look at ya, getting all giddy because your sister's bringing your nephew."

"So?" She stuck her bottom lip out at him.

"Just want to make sure you're not getting any ideas over there." He still hadn't turned to face her but he felt the curiousness in her stare.

"Just because I love spending time with babies doesn't mean I'm ready to be a mother. I know how hard it is raising children, and having a child of my own is the last thing on my mind. They're nice to play with, cute to cuddle, but I know when they get sick or fussy I can just pass them back to their mothers and go do what I wanna do."

Yohan attempted unsuccessfully to hide the smile inching across his lips.

"What are you smiling about?" Krystal asked, crossing her arms over her chest.

He glanced at her from the corner of his eye before replying, "Nothing."

"Oh, uh-uh you gonna tell me what you smiling about."

"And what if I don't?" Yohan changed lanes to catch his exit.

"Let's see." She paused for a moment, contemplating. "Then you really won't have to worry about me getting pregnant," Krystal stated flatly, paying more attention to her nails than to him.

Her expression said it all. Yohan opened his mouth to reply but changed his mind. He didn't want to get into a battle of wits with her. That was a battle he knew for a fact he'd lose. Instead, he chose the honest approach.

"I just thought about a conversation I had with The Trio a few weeks back." The conversation still bothered him. He'd waited for Dre to corner him, but the day had yet to come.

"So y'all been talking about me behind my back?" She sounded none too happy. First the girls, now the guys. This was getting out of hand. She was growing up, and sooner or later they had to let her go.

"Actually, I got grilled about our sex life."

"What!"

"Seems like they've figured out on their own that our relationship has evolved into something more." Yohan figured the guys would talk to her as well. Apparently, he assumed wrong.

"Guess that explains my little girls' night out." She grabbed her lip gloss and applied another coat.

"They got you too?" he replied, unable to control his snickering. He could only imagine what the women had talked about.

"Yep. We spent the whole night talking about respect and taking the necessary precautions; birth control, ya know, the usual 'everyone thinks you're too young to have a baby' speech."

"That's true, you know." He actually agreed with the message, though not necessarily how they'd gone about delivering it.

"Don't you think I know that? Believe me, getting pregnant is the last thing I want to happen. Even though I know you'd stay by my side and support your family. I see what China goes through trying to stay in school, cheerleading, and taking care of Hassan. She's my girl and all, but personally I don't think I could do it."

"If you had to, you could, but I'm glad we agree that a baby is not a good idea at this point." He relaxed, not realizing he'd become tense. They'd had this conversation before, but Yohan was relieved knowing she still felt this way.

"Guess what else?" Krystal teased.

"What?"

"They also taught me a few new tricks. Bet Dre and Brey don't know their women spilled their bedroom habits. Maybe one day I'll show you what I learned."

Yohan didn't like the seductive look Krystal gave him. He knew how women talked. They were worse than men in the locker room when it came to discussing sex. For a moment he thought about asking her to elaborate, but now wasn't a good time and this definitely wasn't a good place. Instead, he chose to just absorb what Krystal was telling him, hoping one day she'd want to share what she'd learned.

Yohan pulled into a parking space and helped Krystal from the truck. The couple walked hand in hand through the terminal door where immediately she dropped his hand and took off in the direction of a short, brown-skinned woman with astonishing long, dark hair. The woman stepped out of the main flow of traffic, placing the car seat with her infant child securely in it on the floor. She smiled widely, seeing her sister running like a madwoman toward her.

Yohan could only shake his head as he made his way through the crowd. He watched Myisha's eyes take him in as he approached.

"There's some dude heading our way," Myisha whispered.

Krystal frowned, not quite understanding what her sister was talking about. She peeped over her shoulder just as Yohan draped his arms over her shoulders.

"Oh, you mean this fine brotha? Myisha, this is my sweetie, Yohan. Yohan, this is my sister, Myisha."

"Hi," Myisha said, giving him a wave. "And that's my little one at your feet staring wide-eyed up at you."

Done with the formalities, Yohan scooped up the car seat and grabbed the bags from Myisha. He walked a few steps ahead of the two women, giving them some privacy to catch up.

"He's definitely a looker," Myisha said to Krystal.

"He's more than a looker," Krystal confessed, her eyes roaming over Yohan's backside. Images of their love-making flashed in her mind, making her smile.

Myisha cut her eyes at her sister. "Oh really? Do tell."

"Not right now. We've got so much to catch up on and plenty of time to talk about Mr. Tall, Dark, and Handsome later when he's not around."

"I heard that," Yohan said, not taking the time to stop or turn around. "Myisha, just remember you can't always believe what people tell you, unless it's good news."

It didn't take long for Myisha to get the little one bathed, fed, and settled into the crib for the night. She joined her sister on the couch and the two women spent the next half an hour just catching up on how Krystal was doing in school and how Myisha's job was going.

Yohan stepped from the bedroom. He watched Krystal and Myisha cackling like a couple of hens on the couch in the living room. Making his way to the couch, he leaned over and pecked Krystal on the cheek.

"Hey, babe, I'm about to head out. You need anything before I go?" He kneaded her shoulders, the desire to touch her overwhelming him.

"Nope. I think we're good." She placed her hands over his. "You doing bank drops tonight?"

"Not that I am aware of. I'll probably be in around

two." Placing one last kiss on her lips, he grabbed his keys from the end table and headed out of the door.

"Out? At this hour?" Myisha gave her sister a suspicious look.

"I know what you're thinking and no, he is not doing anything illegal. The guys who took me in own a club. He usually works there three or four nights a week. Yohan plays security quite well."

"You sure working is all he's doing in the club? I mean, it is Friday night. How many weekends do you stay at home while he's out there doing who knows what?" She leaned forward, resting her arms on her knees. She glared at her sister, waiting for whatever reply Krystal might come up with.

"It's not even like that. During football and basketball season I usually have games on Friday nights. I don't have a license, so anytime I need to be somewhere, he takes me. It just so happens that this week's game is Saturday night. Hey, wanna come?"

"I don't think having an infant at a basketball game is a good idea."

"Oh, I'm sure Aubrey's wife won't mind keeping him for a few hours."

Myisha stared at her sister, not sure about leaving her child with some stranger.

Krystal grabbed the phone from the cradle, prepared to dial the home number of the eldest Fedichi brother.

"I don't know about this. I don't think I'll be comfortable leaving him with a stranger."

"She not a stranger. Come on," Krystal urged. "It'll be fun and you'll get to see your sister in action."

Myisha thought for a moment. It would be nice to have a little time away from the little one. And it would give her a chance to really see how her sister was when she was in her element. She might even get a little alone time with Yohan. Maybe she'd get the chance to find out how Krystal was really doing.

Myisha gave in. Krystal dialed Aubrey's number. She made the babysitting arrangements while Myisha checked on the baby.

Closing the bedroom door, Myisha plopped down in the chair across from her sister. Krystal quickly finished the phone call and turned to see her sister gawking at her.

"I meant to ask you where you got the baby furniture from." She was hoping Krystal wasn't going to tell her she was pregnant.

"It's not what you think. It's borrowed from Aubrey."

"But I thought you said they had a newborn." Myisha straightened the magazines on the coffee table to keep her hands busy. Since giving birth, she'd become accustomed to doing something every waking moment.

"They do." Krystal didn't quite understand the underlying concern her sister showed.

"Then why'd you take the crib?"

"It's a spare. Their house is huge. Aubrey thought it'd be easier if they had two of everything, that way she'd have what she needed no matter where she was."

An awkward silence hung between the two women. Though they talked on the phone at least once a month, seeing Myisha face-to-face, Krystal didn't really know what to say to her. She was sure her sister had plenty of questions, but she seemed hesitant to ask.

"Okay, Myisha, I know you want to, so go ahead and ask."

"I really don't know where to start. I mean . . ." Myisha stood and made her way behind the chair. She leaned over the top, resting her forearms on the plush leather. "I didn't know what to expect when I got here. But now, seeing how much you've grown and matured, I just don't know what to say."

"I told you I'd be taken care of. Jerad wouldn't have left me in the hands of his cousins if he thought they wouldn't do a good job raising me."

"And what about Yohan?"

Krystal leaned into the soft leather of the sofa. She closed her eyes, reliving the wonderful times she'd shared with Yohan over the past four years. He'd opened up a whole new world for her, nurturing her spirit and feeding her soul. A warm tingle spread through her body, filling every pore with a sense of love and comfort as she thought about the way he'd made her feel last night.

"Yohan was a bonus in all of this. He's been wonderful. He's loving, respectful, and supportive. He listens when I need to talk, he holds me when I need a shoulder to cry on. He takes care of me and makes sure I have everything I need."

"He sounds like quite a catch. Do you love him?"

Krystal turned to face Myisha. "Yeah. I do." She smiled, though the gesture was more for herself than her sister.

"Then I'm happy for you." Myisha worried about whether Krystal would ever be able to give her heart to anyone again after what she'd been through with Jerad. She was glad to see her sister had someone in her life that was good to her and for her.

"Speaking of love, what about you?" Krystal interjected.

"What about me?" Myisha replied, taking a seat in the chair.

Krystal wrinkled her nose and twisted her mouth up at her sister. "You know. What's up with you and baby daddy?"

Myisha thought long and hard about the question. Leaving her face expressionless, she struggled to control the excitement fighting to escape her mouth. Checking on Krystal wasn't the only reason she'd decided to take this trip. She also had some news that she wanted to deliver in person.

"Well, that's the other reason I wanted to see my little sister. We're getting married."

Krystal jumped from her seat, pulling her sister into a hug. "That's wonderful. When did he propose?"

"The night Jolon was born. He took one look into his son's eyes and he knew he wanted us to be a real family."

"Aaaawww. So, are you excited? Have y'all set a date? Where are you going to have the wedding? Who—" Krystal sat down again.

"Whoa, slow down, one question at a time."

"Sorry, I'm just so happy for you."

"I'm happy too. I mean . . . all that we've been through and we made it. We really made it. But I do have one concern as far as the wedding goes." The smile drained from Myisha's face.

"What's wrong, Myisha?" Krystal patted her sister on the knee.

"You're going to get upset," she replied, lowering her eyes and eventually her head.

Krystal released a heavy sigh. She knew where this conversation was going.

"Look." Myisha raised her head to look Krystal in the eyes. "I want my baby sister to be there . . . at the wedding. I know you and Mom and Dad haven't exactly seen eye to eye on Jerad, but . . ."

"Wait. Mom and Dad aside, there are some things I think you'll be glad to hear. Come on." Krystal pulled her sister to the couch. She closed her eyes for a moment, sorting through the thoughts racing around her mind. After a moment more of contemplation, she determined the best place to start.

"In all of the time I've been gone, I never opened the

letter Jerad left for me. And up until a little over a month ago, I hadn't told anyone that I was the one who found him."

"Oh my God, Krystal." Myisha pulled her sister into a loving embrace. "Why didn't you tell anyone?"

"Who was I going to tell? I didn't really have any friends I could talk to about it. I couldn't tell Mom and Dad. And you were gone."

"Krystal, I am so sorry." Now, knowing the truth about what she'd concealed the last four years, Myisha continued to hug and rock her sister. She'd had no idea Krystal had found Jerad.

"It's okay. I finally stepped out on faith and opened the letter. I hit rock bottom for a while and there have been days where I wasn't sure life was really worth living, but with the help of Yohan and Jerad's cousins, I'm working through things. I will admit, some days are better than others, but I'm making it. I've even started therapy to deal with Jerad's death."

"I'm proud of you. I'm glad you're dealing with things. You know if you ever need anything, I'm here. You're the only sister I have and I love you."

"I love you too."

Chapter Nineteen

Krystal planted a sloppy, wet kiss on Yohan's lips be-fore she climbed out of the truck to join her sister on the sidewalk.

"I'll call you when we're ready to go." She closed the door and waved good-bye as Yohan pulled away from the curb and turned down one of the aisles in the parking lot.

"So, do you want to shop or eat first?" Krystal asked.

"Why, shop of course."

For the next hour and a half, the two women shopped to their heart's content all at the expense of Aubrey. He'd given Krystal one of the credit cards and told her to buy whatever she or Myisha wanted. The missus was watch-ing Myisha's little one, leaving the two sisters with the freedom to do as they pleased.

They settled down in a corner booth in one of the restaurants in the mall. They both ordered chicken salads so it only took a few minutes for their food to arrive.

"So how are you enjoying your stay?" Krystal asked her sister.

"You know, you've surprised me in so many ways.

You've really turned your life around. I don't think I've seen you this happy since before Jerad died."

"I don't think I've been happy since. I mean, when I first left, things were good. As long as I did well in school and Yohan was with me, I could pretty much do what I wanted. No curfew, I could date, China and I had sleep-overs, Yohan and I went on road trips. I mean, it was great." Krystal's mood changed. The smile dropped from her lips, leaving a touch of sadness in her eyes.

"But?" Myisha watched the joy drain from her sister. In all of the good times, she knew there was more. Krystal had only managed to temporarily run away from the real issue.

"But in the end, Jerad's death still hung over all of the good times. The more fun I had, the more I thought about him, the more I missed him." Krystal closed her eyes, fighting the burning beneath her eyelids. "For a long time, they believed I was all right, that I was okay with everything, but the reality was, all of the anger, sad-ness, and hurt was slowly eating me up inside."

"So what changed?"

Krystal looked up at her sister. "I did. I looked around at the happiness Aubrey and his wife share, the way China looks at Hassan, even the way Dre's girl caters to his needs, and I wanted that. I wanted to be able to give my relationship with Yohan a real chance, and I realized that I've been doing him a disservice. I know what I feel for him, I've known for a long time, but even with all that we've been through, I still held back." There, she'd said it. In her heart she knew that was the reason she was fi-nally able to open the letter. She knew it was time. Time for her to grow up. Time for her to learn the truth. Time for her to let him go.

"I'm glad you're getting your life together."

An expression of bewilderment crossed Krystal's face at her sister's reply. "Spill it, My."

"I just wish you'd at least call Mom and Dad. They call every night asking if I've heard from you. I hate lying to them."

"Then why do you? Why don't you just tell them the truth?"

Myisha just stared at her sister, not sure what to say. She'd never considered just telling them. She knew if she told them they'd come looking for her, but Myisha was still sure Krystal wasn't ready to face their parents. And yet, here she was questioning why she'd never told their parents where she was.

"Never mind, My. You don't have to answer that. I know why you've never told them. And I thank you for that. You've given me the greatest gift at the expense of the honesty I know you value so. I'll make things right, soon. I promise."

Finishing the remainder of their lunch in silence, the two quickly gathered their purchases to meet Yohan at the mall entrance. He helped them load the armfuls of packages into the truck.

Once everyone was settled he asked, "So where to?"

Krystal continued to stare out of the window, absorbed in her own thoughts. Yohan glanced in the rearview mirror to see Myisha doing the same.

"Did something happen that I need to know about?" he asked, more concern in his voice than he intended.

"Huh? Oh, sorry, what did you just say?"

"Talk to me, Krystal." Yohan didn't like the distant look in her eyes. She was hiding something and he wanted to know what.

"It's nothing," she replied, giving him a weak smile. "I've just got some things on my mind. We'd better get back to the house. I've got a game to get ready for."

"You sure you don't want to talk about it? You know you always feel better when you talk."

Krystal glanced over her shoulder before responding, "No. I'm okay."

"What about the baby?"

"Myisha's coming to the game. Aren't you, My?" Immediately, Krystal perked up.

"Yeah." Myisha's head whipped around, her hair quickly following, slapping her in the face. "She twisted my arm."

"We can pick him up after the game."

"If you say so," replied Yohan.

Yohan put the truck in drive and blended in with the slow moving traffic. He'd drop it for now, but sooner or later he intended to find out what was on her mind.

Myisha flipped through the hundreds of television stations trying to distract her mind. Krystal's question had rattled her. Why hadn't she ever told their parents about where she was? She'd had numerous opportunities but for some reason, she always said the same thing when they asked: no.

The more she thought about it, the more confused she became. She thought back to the day Krystal left. Myisha had been sure that if her sister stayed home, she would have gone through with another suicide attempt. She didn't want that for her, so she went along with the plan, hoping Krystal would realize what a big mistake she was making.

But it had been four years now and Myisha wondered why in all of this time Krystal refused to even so much as call home and most of all, why she was questioning why she hadn't told them where she was.

Her mind deep in thought, she didn't hear the two gentlemen enter until one of them closed the front door. Snapping around to face them, she stared wide-eyed at the two men, her eyes darting back and forth between the identical faces.

Yohan turned around in just enough time to keep Myisha from asking the question they all knew was coming.

"Myisha, these are the other two members of The Trio. Andre,"—Andre reached out to shake Myisha's hand—"and Antonio." Antonio did the same. "Guys, this is Krystal's sister, Myisha."

"I see you've met the rest of the crew."

All heads whisked in Krystal's direction as she stepped around the corner leading to the master bedroom.

"A couple of cuties, ain't they?" she commented, smiling at Myisha. "And two of them too. Make you wanna eat them up, don't it?"

"Okay, Krystal, we get the picture. So, are you ready to go?" Dre asked.

"Yep. Come on, My, you can sit between the big strong twins." Krystal pulled her sister between the twins and out of the door.

Once at the game, Myisha settled comfortably between Yohan and Andre. The bleachers were still fairly empty and they had nearly twenty minutes before the game started. Based upon the crowd that had formed behind them in line, she was sure each side would be packed before the end of the girls' game.

"Can I ask you guys a question?" Myisha looked back and forth between the men.

"Sure," Andre replied.

"How is my sister? Really?" She needed to know. Krystal had spent so much of her life pretending everything was copacetic that Myisha wasn't sure she knew the difference.

"She's come a long way from that first night my brothers and I came and got her. It took her some time to adjust, but she's been in good hands. We know Jerad wanted the best for her, and that's all we've ever wanted for her as well. We're still working on her emotional well-being, but she's determined not to let anything stand in her way. As a matter of fact, if she stays on track,"— Andre eyed Yohan, making sure he caught the not-so-subtle warning—"she'll graduate at the top of her class. Krystal's smart. And she's strong. She'll get through this, just like she's gotten through so many other obstacles in her life."

Andre turned his attention back to Krystal. He thought back to all she'd been through in the last few months and he just prayed she'd be strong enough to continue to improve.

"I'm glad she's doing well, but what I really need to know is if she's happy."

"She's learning how to be," Yohan answered. If anyone knew about her happiness it was him.

"What do you mean?" Myisha asked, shifting her focus from Andre to Yohan. She watched the love in his eyes as he explained.

"She's beginning to understand what happiness is. She's beginning to let go of the hurt she's kept in her heart for so long. She found true love at such a young age that when it was lost to her, she didn't know how to let go. But now, as each day passes, she smiles a little more. She's doing the little things she hasn't done since Jerad was in her life and she's enjoying every minute of it."

"You really do love her, don't you?"

Yohan faced Myisha as he said the words. "I love her more than life itself, and I'll do anything in my power to protect her and bring her happiness. I know you'll be going home in a couple of days, but know that your sister's in good hands."

Myisha took comfort in Yohan's words. Her sister appeared well and seemed happy and at this point in Krystal's life, that's what she needed the most.

Chapter Twenty

An uneasy silence hung between Krystal and Myisha as the sisters entered the airport. Yohan, only a few steps behind them, carried the car seat in one had and pulled Myisha's rolling luggage with the other. He'd listened to the friendly banter of the two sisters during the drive to the airport and they'd seemed happy enough. Yet when they reached the parking lot, the giddy chatter seeped into a not-so-subtle silence.

Yohan and Krystal waited while Myisha checked her baggage. Krystal spent the few minutes shaking the blue-and-white rattle above her nephew's head, watching as the little boy's eyes filled with glee.

"You okay?" Yohan asked as he rocked the car seat with his foot.

"Yeah. I am."

Myisha joined them in the crowded terminal. "Can I speak with my sister for a minute?"

Yohan had the feeling that whatever it was Myisha wanted to discuss with Krystal had something to do with Krystal's relationship with their parents. The last couple of days he'd overheard them talk about what it was like growing up when they were both still living at home. Yohan hadn't realized how close Krystal had been to her sister, or at least from her point of view how much she looked up to Myisha. He thought it was a shame that they had waited so long to visit in person.

"We'll be over there when you two are done." Yohan grabbed the car seat and cut his way through the crowd, taking a seat in a corner next to a newsstand.

"How about some white hot chocolate?" Myisha asked as she dragged her sister in the direction of a coffee shop a few feet from the start of the security checkpoint maze. They each slid into a seat across from one another at a little metal table against the back wall of the seating area.

"So you really going to try to work things out with Mom and Dad?" Myisha stared into her cup of hot chocolate. For some reason she couldn't bring herself to look at her sister when she asked the question.

"My." Krystal stared at her sister. "My, look at me." Myisha's gaze traveled from the steaming cup to her sister's caring eyes. "I'm not going to make any promises about going home. I can't say for sure that everything is going to be perfect again for our family, but I can promise you that no matter what, come next year, I will be there to see my only sister walk down the aisle. Besides, you gonna need someone to watch Little Man while Mommy and Daddy celebrate."

"Oh, Krystal." No longer able to control her happiness, Myisha leaned across the table to hug her sister. Though she nearly knocked over both of their drinks, she just had to let Krystal know how happy she was.

Yohan, clearing his throat, drew their attention away from their moment of sisterly bonding. "I hate to interrupt, but Little Man needs to be changed and I don't have the diaper bag."

Myisha wiped the tears from her eyes. "I'll go take care of him." Slinging the diaper bag over her shoulder, Myisha grabbed the car seat.

"Wait, My. You two need to get going anyway." Krystal waited while Myisha put the car seat back on the floor next to their table. "Besides it's getting late and this one"—she pointed at Yohan—"has to work tonight."

The sisters embraced again, taking one last moment to pass secret memories that they'd discovered over the last two days. The end of this trip had been eventful and emotional for the both of them, but it had erased the years since they'd last seen each other. That missing time didn't matter anymore. They were on the road to fixing their family and at that moment, that was all that mattered.

"Call me when you guys get back in and settled. I don't care what time it is."

"I will. And don't forget I love you."

"Love you too, My."

Yohan wrapped his fingers around Krystal's as they watched Myisha head in the direction of the bathroom. "Ready to go home?"

"Yeah, I am. And thanks for these last few days. I appreciated you giving me some time with my sister."

"I think you two needed it." He held her close. She felt different to him, but he couldn't quite place the feeling. He'd have to remember to ask her tomorrow.

Hours after dropping off Myisha and her son at the airport, wetness running down her cheeks drew Krystal from a troublesome sleep. Before she opened her eyes, the image of Yohan's truck rolling over in a ditch flashed before her. She rolled over in bed, reaching for him, sure he was beside her. Instead, she only felt the coolness of the undisturbed sheets.

Flipping on the lamp, she grabbed the cordless phone

and dialed his cell. Her foot tapped vigorously as she waited for him to pick up the phone. She released a sigh of relief the minute she heard his voice.

"Krystal, what's wrong?" Yohan asked with concern in his voice. It was nearly four-thirty in the morning and her calling at this hour was more than disturbing.

"Thank God you're alive."

"What are you talking about?"

"I had another dream." Almost out of breath from the panic, she continued. "I saw your truck get run off the road."

"Fuck!" he yelled, standing up to find Aubrey.

"What is it?"

Krystal listened as Yohan told Brey they needed to find Tonio. "Yohan! Yohan, what's going on?" she yelled into the phone.

"Listen, Krystal, I don't want to alarm you, but Tonio took my truck."

"Oh no. Please no." Krystal almost dropped the phone as her hand started to shake.

"Don't worry, baby. Everything's going to be fine. Aubrey and I are heading out right now. Brey knows where he went. We'll find him. I promise. I'll call you as soon as we locate him. Okay?"

"Okay." Krystal's mind hung in a fog as she sat by the phone waiting. She tried to call Antonio, Aubrey, Andre, and even Yohan, but no one answered their phones.

Krystal felt so helpless. She needed to do something, but she didn't know what. Grabbing her journal from the end table, she filled the pages with the emotions occupying her body and mind. Halfway through the fourth page, the sound of the lock on the front door turning pulled her attention from the thoughts on the paper. With his head hung low, Yohan entered their home.

"Go put on some clothes. I told them I'd bring you to the hospital," he said without looking up at her.

"Is he . . ." Her words trailed off as the thought that he may already be dead made its presence known.

"He's still alive, but he's in pretty bad shape."

Krystal threw on the first thing she found: some jeans and a sweatshirt. Removing a scrunchie from the dresser, she tied her hair in a ponytail. She grabbed her purse from the chaise and joined Yohan in the living room.

He looked up at her. If Tonio didn't pull through, he'd have to be strong for her. But he wasn't sure he had it in him. Though he hid his feelings, he was hurting as much as she was.

They found the others in the waiting room adjacent to the ER of Crawford Long Hospital. Andre was stretched out in one of the chairs, staring at the ceiling. Aubrey stood with his back turned to the entrance, engrossed in something outside of the window. The sun had risen nearly an hour ago and the additional light warmed the air in the waiting area.

Krystal took the seat next to Andre as Yohan approached Aubrey. Dre turned to see fresh tears forming in her eyes. He covered her hand with his, giving it a gentle squeeze. Neither knew what to say to the other, so they chose to remain silent. Keeping their respective thoughts to themselves, they both hoped and prayed Antonio would pull through.

"Any news?" Yohan asked Aubrey.

"Not a word. He's still in surgery. Besides the head injury, he's got some broken ribs and a collapsed lung." Brey continued to stare out the window.

"Any idea who did this?"

"None. Somebody hit him, though. There was red

paint on the rear quarter panel. He was pushed into that ditch." He balled his fist as anger replaced worry. The more he tried to piece this together, the more fucked-up he realized this was.

"The question is why?"

"I have no idea. I do suspect that this was personal. None of the money was missing. Not only that, whoever did this must have followed him from the club."

Aubrey explained to Yohan that the route Antonio took tonight was by all accounts deserted at night. Not even the drug dealers traveled that road after three A.M. Most of the streets he took circled the perimeter of Lincoln Heights, so unless you lived in the area, you didn't even know they existed. Aubrey was sure whoever was responsible for running Antonio off of the road had to have followed him.

Suddenly, the door swung open and a woman in green scrubs entered the crowded area. She scanned the room looking for the family of her patient. Her complexion paled the moment her eyes stopped on Andre. She looked as if she'd seen a ghost.

Aubrey and Yohan gathered around as the doctor approached.

"You all must be Mr. Fedichi's family?"

She never took her eyes off of Andre. He was used to the reaction. Other than his eyes being dark brown and Antonio's hazel, he and his twin were identical.

"Is he going to make it?" Aubrey asked.

The doctor looked up at the other face sharing the features of her patient. Though a year older than his twin brothers, Aubrey shared all of their facial features.

The woman released a sigh before responding. "We're not sure. We've done all we can for him. It's touch and go from here. We had to put a tube in his head to relieve the pressure. He's in a coma but appears to have plenty of brain activity. The next twenty-four to forty-eight hours are critical. We just have to wait and see what happens."

"Can we see him?"

"They're moving him to the ICU. Once he's settled in there you should be able to see him."

Krystal could no longer contain her sorrow. She let it all out with one heartbreaking wail. Andre wrapped his arms around her, allowing her to cry into his chest. She took the news the hardest, probably because of her dream. Yohan took a seat next to her, not knowing how to help her. Aubrey rubbed her back as she screamed and cried and beat her fist into Andre's chest. Andre just held on to her, helpless to take away her sorrow, but knowing he couldn't let her go.

Chapter Twenty-one

Minutes turned to hours, hours to days, days to weeks. Krystal remained by Antonio's bedside as much as possible. The first few days in the ICU she was only allowed to visit in short intervals. Those days were the hardest on his family. Krystal wouldn't eat, and she didn't sleep much. Between the spells of tears, she stared out of the waiting room window. Yohan spent most of his time worried about her, while Andre and Brey paced and filtered phone calls.

By the second week, though, Antonio was in a regular room and the doctors continued to say he was improving each day. The swelling in his head had reduced significantly and the puffiness around his eyes subsided. The doctors had removed the tube from his head and even allowed Aubrey to cut his hair.

However, with the good news came the bad. Antonio had a history of respiratory infections and a moderate case of asthma. He'd contracted pneumonia, which ultimately resulted in him being placed on a ventilator. And he still hadn't opened his eyes.

The doctors kept telling them it may take some time. An injury as severe as the one Antonio managed to live through was traumatic for the body. "When he's ready he'll open them," the nurses continued to tell Krystal. She had her doubts, though. The best specialists money could buy had seen Antonio, and not one of them was able to say with any certainty if or when he might open his eyes.

She longed to see the two light brown pools delicately placed in a sea of white staring back at her. She missed the way the light danced around in them. She remembered the night at the club when they'd caught her with Octavio how his eyes held anger and disappointment while still remaining warm and caring.

She turned from the birds gathered at the windowsill to look over at the peacefully resting Antonio. His body shifted in the bed, releasing the first conscious sign of life she'd seen in far too long.

"Tonio? Tonio, can you hear me?" she called out to him. She made her way to his bedside praying that he'd open his eyes.

He turned his head ever so slightly at the sound of her voice. Then, he finally did it, the one gesture she'd been waiting for. Slowly he opened his eyes.

Krystal smiled as she stared into his eyes. They rolled around in an unnatural movement for a moment, peeking in and out from under the eyelids. He hadn't seen light in nearly two weeks as his mind trapped his body in a state of waiting. After a minute or two more his gaze met with hers.

The tubes from the ventilator made it impossible to speak, so he did the next best thing: slowly turning his hand over, his eyes followed the movement of her hand to his. She intertwined his fingers with hers and a sense of relief passed through her body as he gave her hand a gentle squeeze.

Krystal watched as the corner of his mouth turned up in as much of a smile as he could manage. With her free hand, she wiped the lone tear trailing its way down his cheek. Then, without warning, Antonio closed his eyes, his body relaxing into the bed, his fingers hanging limp against hers as they slipped one by one from her grasp.

Krystal shook her head as she stepped back from him, only stopping when the wall no longer allowed passage. One by one the machines cried out. The lines once indicating his heart rate remained as flat as freshly folded linen. The numbers now read zero. Krystal wanted to call for help but found she couldn't move. She couldn't think, she couldn't react, and most of all she couldn't breathe.

Nurses, doctors, any and everyone rushed into the room. Krystal remained oblivious to the chaos around her. All she could do was stare at Antonio's lifeless body lying against the cold white sheets surrounded by tubes and stainless steel. The next thing she knew, a nurse was escorting her out of the room and everything went black.

Krystal eventually opened her eyes to Yohan hovering over her. "What happened?" she asked.

"You blacked out."

"Oh my God. Antonio. Is he . . ." her voice trailed off. She couldn't bring herself to say the words.

"They're still working on him," Aubrey replied, not looking her in the face.

She leaned up, realizing they were again in one of the hospital waiting rooms. Andre sat in one of the chairs rocking uncontrollably and mumbling something she couldn't understand.

"What's wrong with Dre?" she asked Yohan.

"We don't know. He was pacing a little while ago. He's been like that since he sat down."

Krystal made her way over to Andre. She wrapped her arms around him. "Dre, what's wrong?"

"He can't breathe, Krystal! He's suffocating. He's dying, Krystal, he's dying." Dre grabbed hold of the sleeves of her jacket.

"How do you know?"

He turned his fist as if in pain. The gesture tightened his grip on her and nearly pulled the jacket from her shoulders. "I can feel it. I can feel him slipping away. I can feel him taking a part of me with him."

Krystal held on to him, just as he'd held on to her when she'd first arrived at the hospital. He rocked in her arms, his face full of sorrow and pain. He kept repeating how much it hurt. Then, for no apparent reason, he took in a deep breath and released it. The rocking, the mumbling, the tears, everything just stopped. The world around them became a quiet place and Andre relaxed.

Moments later, the door to the waiting room swung open and the doctor stepped through. Though he'd calmed down, Andre kept his face buried in Krystal's arms and chest and he continued to hold onto her sleeves for dear life.

"I'm sorry, guys. He's gone."

Aubrey's hand reached for the closest chair as his legs gave way. Yohan just stared at the man in disbelief. But this time, Andre was the most upset. He didn't say a word, he just pushed Krystal away and stormed to the door.

"Dre! Dre!" Yohan yelled as he chased after Andre through the door and out into the hallway.

Krystal felt her eyes glaze over as she somehow managed to make her way over to where Aubrey now sat.

"He already knew," she said to him.

"What?"

"He felt it. He felt it all, Aubrey. He lived through each moment of Antonio's death."

Krystal could only stare at him. It hadn't sunk in yet. She kept waiting on something to happen, for that little light in her head to click on at the realization that he was gone. But there was nothing, emptiness, quiet, just nothing. Aubrey wrapped his arm around Krystal, pulling her close. She needed a shoulder to cry on and he needed to feel useful.

Chapter Twenty-two

Bodies lined the pews of the cathedral from wall to wall in the upper and lower levels of the sanctuary. Just as many people huddled around television screens in the classrooms in the adjoining buildings and lounge areas. The air hung heavy with sorrow. The sound of "His Eye is on the Sparrow" surrounded those whose faces no longer reflected the joy Antonio had brought to their lives. They were all here: Mothers, fathers, aunts, uncles, grandparents, children, friends, and family gathered in this place to pay their last respects and say their final good-byes to a young man taken before his prime. Antonio had touched so many lives, made the difference in most of them by taking the time to tend to the little things.

The old folks rocked in their seats, the music reminding them of what church used to be like out in the country on Easter morning, fans flapping, feet stomping, the sounds of the deacon's *amens* slicing through the country heat. The children stared wide-eyed at their mothers, wondering why the water ran from their eyes and why they looked so sad. But their eyes, all of their eyes, remained fixated on the pearl white and gold-trimmed casket surrounded by white and yellow roses and peace lilies, perched in front of the pulpit just beyond the two empty pews with white ribbons tied to the side.

No one turned as the two heavy doors at the back swung open, the air sucked out into the hallway like the last desperate breath of a beached whale. Their attention remained focused on the front of the church. Not even the sound of Krystal's sniffling could break the spell of grief cast over this place.

Antonio's closest friends filed by his casket, only taking quick glances and saying short prayers before sliding into the empty second pew. Aubrey trudged past his baby brother's casket, only glimpsing over at the lifeless body out of the corner of his eye. He stopped in front of the picture on the easel near the head of the coffin. They'd taken the photograph the day before they'd delivered the first truck from the shop. It was that day that they knew the business would be a success.

Aubrey turned again, prepared to take a seat, but found he couldn't move. He only had strength enough to watch the profile of Andre as he stared down into the face of his twin lying in a coffin in the white three-piece double-breasted suit he loved so much. Though he was a few steps away, Aubrey could still clearly see the tears slide down his brother's cheek.

He watched as Andre turned to face him, his eyes asking how were they going to make it now that the voice of reason was gone. He didn't know how to answer his brother's silent plea. All he could do was try to be strong and offer the support they'd all need. As he closed the short distance between them, Aubrey watched Andre again turn to stare down at the brother he'd shared his entire life with. Aubrey's hand on his shoulder gave Dre the strength he needed to say his final good-bye and turn from the face so much like his own.

Taking their place on the front pew, the two brothers watched as Yohan whispered something into Krystal's ear. He raised her chin, gazing into her eyes as he mouthed the words, *you can do this*, to her. He intertwined his fingers with hers, sharing his strength with her. She took one last deep breath before walking the four longest steps of her life.

A sense of loss washed over her when she looked down into Antonio's butterscotch face for the last time. So many memories flooded her mind. Most of them were from happy times, him at her cheerleading competitions cheering her on, the lectures he'd give her about demanding respect as a woman, even the time she'd snuck out and gotten locked out of the house when he'd let her stay. She'd miss his lectures. She'd miss his corny jokes that always made her laugh; but most of all, she'd miss those light brown eyes that could stare into the soul to find the good in everyone.

Krystal reached out, wanting to cradle his face, pull him close, and hold him one last time. The longer she stared at him, the less it seemed like he belonged in the casket. Her breath caught a moment, her mind betraying her as she swore she saw him take a breath. She felt Yohan wrap an arm around her waist the moment she swayed. She turned, burying her face in his chest, bursting into tears.

Yohan looked over at Aubrey, not knowing what to do for Krystal. Aubrey and Andre helped her to the first pew, giving Yohan a moment to speak his piece. He didn't need much time. He and Antonio had been like brothers these last few years. He only had a few last words before he'd be at peace.

"Always thought you'd be standing over my cold

dead body, not the other way around. Guess we were both right about life not being fair. I know you standing up in heaven watching over us. Just know, I'll take care of Krystal. And one last thing, I love you, man."

Though he'd said the words in a hushed voice, Aubrey, Andre, and Krystal heard every word. She reached out to Yohan, beckoning him to take his rightful place with the rest of the family, Antonio's family, his family.

"Brother Fedichi wouldn't want us here today mourning his passing from this life into the next. He'd want us here rejoicing his going home and celebrating the life and joy he's given to so many others. . . ."

The bishop's words slipped from Krystal's consciousness somewhere between the sobs surrounding her, the rocking in Yohan's arms, and Antonio's eyes boring into her soul from the picture. The world around her stood still, no sound, no taste, no breath, just a soothing calm running through her body. She could hear Antonio talking to her. He kept saying it's beautiful in the place he'd gone and that he'd always be with her, watching over her, making sure she was safe. She relaxed against Yohan's chest as she heard Antonio's last words to her: *everything's going to be all right.*

The hustle and bustle in Andre's apartment lasted nearly three hours after Antonio's body was laid to its final rest. People coming in and out, dropping off food, sharing their condolences to let them know how much the people in the community truly loved Antonio. As the last of the mourners walked out of the door, Andre exited Krystal's bedroom. The significant others of the remaining members of The Trio moved around the kitchen dividing up the food left by friends and neighbors, which left Aubrey and his associates in the living room to handle some final business.

The men in this room controlled a number of high-class establishments ranging from banks to restaurants, car dealerships to grocery stores spread throughout the city. Though how the start-up money was made was never addressed, the members of this elite group were all the descendants of long lines of powerful men and women. Beyond business, they'd become a tight-knit family, and The Trio had learned everything they knew about business and protecting family from the other men in the room.

"How is she?" Aubrey asked his brother, resting his head on the back of the chair and closing his eyes.

"Totally freaked out. I gave her two more pills and she's finally asleep." Andre claimed the one remaining empty seat, resting his body for the first time in days. "Where's Yohan?"

"Don't know. I haven't seen him since we got here."

"I think I know where he is. Can y'all finish this without me?" Andre lifted his weary body from the comfort of the chair. He knew Yohan needed some time alone, but right now was the worst time for him to sink into his solitude.

Aubrey raised an eyebrow as he watched his brother leave the apartment.

"Where's he going?"

Aubrey's attention turned in the direction of his mentor, Raffaele. The man exuded power and confidence even in this time of sorrow.

"Probably to Tonio's place," Aubrey replied.

"How is he taking things?" Raffaele perched his fingers in a miniature tepee. He drummed the tips together, deep in thought.

"I don't really know. He's been staying busy, and I know he's worried sick about Krystal. I think he's just taking things one day at a time just like the rest of us."

After a moment more of silence, Raffaele asked, "Still no ideas who did this?"

"No. We're still trying to trace the paint. I'm hoping we can at least get a trace on the type of vehicle it came from."

"Nobody saw anything?" Raffaele wasn't sure that tracing the paint was going to help. Even if they discovered what type of vehicle it came from, the odds of locating that one vehicle were almost none.

"No one's come forward. But he was driving the back roads, so I'm not really surprised."

"We'll find out who did this. And I swear before the first blade of grass grows on Antonio's grave, whoever did this will pay."

Aubrey couldn't think about this anymore. His family was slowly falling apart and he didn't have the slightest idea how to stop it. He'd taught Yohan how to keep a family together, but none of his lessons seemed to fit their current situation.

Andre pushed open the door to Antonio's apartment. He followed the soft glow around the corner of the short hallway at the entrance. He fought back tears as the hypnotic scent of Jamaican rum wrapped around him. Antonio's house always smelled like the islands and being here only brought back memories.

"It's hard to believe he's gone," Dre said as he sat down in the dining room chair across from Yohan.

Yohan didn't look up at him; he just continued to flip through the pages of the photo albums spread across the mahogany table.

"Krystal's finally asleep," he said, hoping to pull Yohan's attention from the pictures. Still the man across from him didn't say a word.

Then, for no apparent reason, Yohan pushed the albums off of the table in one big swoop. He grabbed the chair he'd been sitting in and flung it across the room. It shattered as it impacted with the wall.

Andre tackled him before he could get a good grip on the next chair. It took everything in him, but somehow he managed to wrestle Yohan to the floor.

His mind heavy, his body tired, Yohan lay perfectly still on the floor beneath Andre. So many thoughts raced through his mind, but he didn't have time to sort through them. He needed to get it together. He had a new life now, new responsibilities, and new expectations. He refused to start off like this.

Somehow he managed to pull himself together. "Let me up," he spoke in a calm tone.

Andre looked him over one good time before shifting his weight so that Yohan could get up. They picked themselves up off of the floor, neither looking in the direction of the other.

"I'll come back and clean up the mess I made," Yohan said, picking up the pictures scattered around the room.

"Don't worry about it. Brey and I will take care of it."

"What are y'all going to do with his stuff?"

"I'm not sure. We haven't thought that far out. You're welcome to take whatever you want, and I'm sure there are some things Krystal will probably want. We'll wait until she's well enough to face this before we start to sort through his things." Dre plopped down on the sofa and propped his feet up on the coffee table.

"Still no luck in figuring out who did this?"

"None. I'm sure Brey and the others are doing the best they can. We'll find who did this and he'll pay with his life."

"Still think this was intentional?"

"Don't have any clues otherwise. Why?" Dre narrowed his eyes at Yohan's question. He'd been dancing around this situation for a couple of days, like he may know something more about the situation.

"Nothing. Never mind." Yohan had his suspicions. The red paint, the fact that it was his truck, all clues pointing to him being the target and Antonio caught in the wrong place at the wrong time.

The more he thought about it, the more he was convinced Antonio's death was a case of mistaken identity. Antonio had told him to watch his back, and the red paint was more than just a coincidence. He thought about saying something but decided to keep his suspicions to himself until he had more to go on.

"I guess I'd better get back to Krystal."

"Listen." Dre stopped him before he reached the other side of the room. "Take some time, clear your head, do what you need to do. Brey and I can handle things for a while. We'll make sure Krystal is taken care of."

"No. I need to keep busy. I'm straight." Yohan turned and made his way to the door. A moment later it creaked on its hinges and closed with a thud.

Andre wasn't convinced that Yohan was all right, but right now there was nothing he could do. He just laid his head back and closed his eyes thinking about how things were going to be from now on without his brother. An emptiness filled him, like a part of him had been ripped away, and it probably had, but they'd get through this. Somehow, some way, they'd all get through it.

Chapter Twenty-three

Andre pulled into the parking spot next to Yohan's truck in front of their apartment building. Yohan sat in silence, engrossed in his thoughts as Andre removed the key from the ignition.

"You cool, man?" Andre asked.

He and Aubrey were beginning to worry about Yohan. Since Antonio's death, he'd been withdrawn. He kept busy, taking over the bank drops and most of Antonio's responsibilities at the wheel shop, but they'd yet to see him really mourn Antonio's death.

"Huh?" Yohan shook his mind into clarity. "Yeah, I'm straight." He didn't turn to face Andre. Instead, he reached for the door handle and pulled.

Yohan climbed out of the truck. Shifting his attention to the dark apartment above them, he wondered how Krystal was doing. It was nearly two in the morning and he figured she was in bed asleep by now. Stepping onto the sidewalk, the scent of marijuana drifted into his nostrils. He glanced over at Andre, trying to determine if he'd smelled it too, but Dre was a few paces ahead of him and making his way to the stairwell without hesitation.

Following the intensity of the smell, Yohan turned again to face the balcony of his apartment. The silhouette of a pair of size five white tennis shoes caught his attention. As his stare lingered a moment more, he caught a glimpse of the orange tip of what he assumed was a blunt rising in the darkness, glowing a little brighter, then again dropping out of his sight. The scent of the herb intensified as the expelled smoke floated in the wind. Fighting back anger, Yohan narrowed his eyes.

"Yohan! Yohan!"

The sound of Andre calling his name broke Yohan's concentration. "What!" he yelled back, the word more of a statement than a question.

"You coming?" Dre asked, curious as to why Yohan was standing in the middle of the sidewalk staring up at his apartment. He hadn't been himself in a number of days and his current actions didn't sit well with Dre.

Yohan finally turned and made his way to the stairwell, joining Andre near the bottom.

"I'll catch up with you in a minute. I'm'a stop in and check on Krystal." He took the stairs two at a time in a mad attempt to release his anger. He was sure his eyes and nose hadn't betrayed him, but he needed to see the act to know for sure.

Yohan closed the door to the apartment he shared with Krystal just as Andre reached the top of the stairs. Dre hesitated a moment, thinking he smelled weed when he passed. Laughing at himself, knowing good and well he was the only weed smoker in the building, he put one foot in front of the other toward the end of the hallway where his apartment sat waiting.

* * *

Instead of slamming the door, Yohan pushed it just enough for the lock to catch. Krystal showed no sign of hearing his conversation with Andre, so he figured she either had her headphones on or the radio in the bedroom up. The blaring of the stereo confirmed his suspicion as he slipped into the bedroom.

He reached to turn the radio down then decided against it. He stood in awe, watching her take puff after puff from the spliff. He fought a battle in his mind, trying to determine whether to confront her now or wait until she was done. He reached over to flip on the lamp, then changed his mind. Again he reached for the radio only to stop himself before turning the knob. His eyes never wavered from the orange glow as it rose, intensified, dulled and again dropped to the side of the chair.

Yohan's ears burned as anger replaced distrust, disbelief, and disappointment. Taking in a deep breath, his mind counted backward from ten. With each number, he calmed. By the time he reached one, the burning sensation in his ears ceased, the tension in his hands released, and a newfound confidence to handle this situation tactfully engulfed him. First things first, though. He turned the volume knob on the stereo to zero, and then he flipped on the lamp.

Krystal nearly jumped from her seat, realizing someone was in the apartment. She wasn't expecting Yohan home for at least another couple of hours, giving her time to finish her spliff, air out the apartment, and burn some incense to cover the smell. To her surprise, though, he stood before her, face heavy with disappointment, arms crossed over his chest, awaiting an answer to an unspoken question.

She tried to maintain her composure, putting out the remaining portion of the spliff in the ashtray. She stood, brushing off the bits of tobacco from the cigar she'd split open to roll the weed. She faced him, returning his glare, waiting for him to ask the question she was sure was on the tip of his tongue.

Tired of staring her down, knowing she wanted him to make the first move, in the calmest voice he could muster Yohan asked, "What the hell do you think you're doing?"

"What do you care?" she spat at him.

He bit his tongue to keep from saying the first words that came to his mind. This situation dictated he remain civil. He understood she had a lot to contend with and he'd try to be as understanding as humanly possible.

"What is that supposed to mean?"

"It means exactly what it says." Krystal's neck rolling and pout clearly indicated that she thought her actions were justified.

"Why are you doing this, Krystal?"

"What am I doing, Yohan? Huh? Living my life, coping the best way I know how to cope. Lately, I've been doing just fine on my own, not that I've had much choice." Rolling her eyes, she turned her back to him.

"So you consider smoking weed coping?"

"I do what I have to do. No thanks to you."

"Why are you so angry with me?" A startled response he expected, even her falling apart, crying or trying to hide what she was doing possibly, but he never anticipated her outright defiance. Not to mention the anger directed at him.

"If you don't know, I'm not going to tell you."

Yohan froze at the rage-laced words. He flexed his hands, resisting the urge to slap some sense into her. He found himself fighting his anger more and more since Antonio's passing. He tried patience, he tried understanding, but Krystal just kept pushing. Yohan counted backward from ten and when he reached one, he started again.

"Fuck it." He turned from her, the need to get as far away as possible negating all other thoughts, needs, movements.

"Yohannes Doran Hampton, don't you dare turn your back on me!"

Two steps from the bedroom door rage overcame him and before he realized it, the thin white sheetrock gave way to his fist. Pulling his hand from the hole, he rubbed the white powder from his knuckles. He didn't turn to face her when he said the words, but he made sure she heard him loud and clear.

"Ya know, you're not the only one around here going through shit." He lowered his head before continuing. He needed to say what was on his mind, but he knew the minute he did, things between them would deteriorate significantly. "It seems to me I can't do anything right for you anymore."

"So what are you saying?"

"I'm saying I've done all I can for you."

"Well, since I've been doing this on my own, maybe I should be on my own."

"If that's what you want, then do what you gotta do. It's not like you don't have anywhere to go." His back remained turned to her as his shoulders slumped, weighed with an overwhelming sense of defeat. He hated losing her, but he didn't have anything left to give. She'd taken all of the fight out of him.

"Fine." She snatched her keys from the nightstand, her purse and book bag from the chair, and with her head held high, she walked right past him out of the bedroom.

The sound of the front door slamming pierced his heart, leaving a sense of finality lingering in the air. He loved her so much and he hated to see her hurting, but there was nothing he could do. His pain took refuge in his heart and until he faced it, it was useless trying to help her with hers.

Overcome with sorrow, Yohan somehow managed to light the remaining weed Krystal had moments before extinguished in the makeshift ashtray. Other than the occasional cigar, Yohan felt no need to smoke. He'd witnessed what drugs did to his father, and far too many of his friends started out smoking marijuana, only to move on to other, more potent drugs when the effects no longer suited them.

None of that mattered tonight, though. Slowly but surely the layers of his life one by one peeled away like the skin of an orange. His best friend now lay in a cold, silent grave and his woman retreated to a place not unknown to him but still just out of his grasp. Yohan squeezed his eyes shut to fight away the tears. His sanity still lingered in the present, though he wasn't sure for how long.

Krystal walked the neighborhood for nearly an hour trying to clear her conscience. Though she felt bad about the way she'd said it, she meant every word she spoke to him. Since the day she'd watched Antonio give up on life, dealing with his death consumed her.

She circled around to the front of her building. As she walked past Andre's truck, she was surprised to see Yohan's gone. Rolling her eyes, she made her way up the stairs. She only hesitated a moment in front of her apartment door before deciding to continue down the hall to Andre's place.

Andre pressed pause on his game controller at the sound of a key inserting into the lock. Though he expected Yohan at any moment, he didn't have a key, and Andre seriously doubted Aubrey would be at his door this late. Sliding his hand beneath the sofa pillows, he prepared to draw on any intruder who may have gained access to a set of keys.

His finger slipped from the safety of his pistol when Krystal flung the front door open with so much force he was sure a hole would remain where the knob made contact with the wall. She closed it with just as much anger, causing the dishes in the kitchen cabinets to rattle. He watched a raging Krystal walk right past him without acknowledging his existence. The scent of marijuana followed in the air behind her. She entered the bedroom she'd claimed as her own the first night she came to Lincoln Heights, and slammed the door shut behind her.

Andre stared at the closed door, trying to decide whether he should try to talk to Krystal now or let her cool off. After a short contemplation, he decided to give her some time. Meanwhile, he'd go have a talk with Yohan to find out what had just transpired between them.

He knocked on the door and rang the bell to Krystal and Yohan's apartment, but no one answered. He walked down the stairs to the parking lot only to discover Yohan's truck gone. He tried to call, but only the sound of voice mail taunted him on the other line. Apparently neither of them wanted to talk about what happened.

Chapter Twenty-four

Though the therapist's office remained full of the same cheerfulness it always held, the soothing calm Krystal normally felt here refused to comfort her. She stared out of the window across the room, watching as a light drizzle coated the leaves of the Bradford pear trees. She channeled her thoughts in a positive direction, singing childish nursery rhymes in her head to keep the tears at bay.

Andre, placing his hand over hers, drew her attention for a moment and for the first time since they'd arrived, she turned saddened eyes to him. She forced a weak smile, attempting to assure him she was glad for his support. Normally Yohan would be by her side at therapy, but he hadn't come into work and wasn't answering the phone, so here she was again dealing with Antonio's death without the support of the one person she needed it from.

"Are you sure you're up to this today?" Andre reached up, wiping away the tears running down Krystal's cheeks. She didn't look well at all. She hadn't been eating, and the last few nights he heard her walking through the apartment at all hours.

"No, but I need to figure out how to deal with this."

Before he could respond the office door opened and the doctor stepped in. "Well, hello you—" The woman expected to see Krystal with Yohan. Instead, taken off guard by the unfamiliar face, she stopped halfway through her greeting.

"May I speak with you outside for a moment?" Dre asked, standing and eventually walking past the woman out into the hallway.

Krystal nodded her agreement, assuring the good doctor that she had no problem with her speaking with Andre.

"We won't be long."

The doctor turned and Krystal watched as the door closed behind her.

"I know you were probably expecting Yohan, and any other time he'd be here, but we've recently lost a family member and—"

"Wait." She wanted to make sure she completely understood the situation before he continued. "Did Krystal lose Yohan?"

"No. My brother Antonio was murdered a few weeks ago. He and Yohan were pretty close. I don't know what happened between him and Krystal, but they haven't spoken in a few days. I just thought you should know."

"Does she want you to stay with her during our session?"

"I didn't ask." Dre's eyes darted in the direction of the closed door before he looked back over at the doctor. He didn't mind staying, but this was Krystal's time and he wanted her to be comfortable, so the decision was hers.

"Wait here. I'll talk to her." The doctor entered her office, pulling the door closed behind her. "Krystal . . ."

"I don't want him to hear." Krystal had already decided she didn't want Andre in on their session today. She didn't want him worrying about her any more than he already was, and after what she planned to talk about today, she was sure he'd worry.

Krystal stared at the woman as she stuck her head out into the hallway. Though she tried, she couldn't make out the words the woman said to Dre. One thing she was positive of, though, was that he wasn't going to be happy about not being allowed to sit in on her session.

"Krystal." The doctor claimed the seat across from Krystal. Normally she'd sit behind her desk taking notes, but the gesture felt too impersonal and right now she was sure Krystal was looking for someone to be more of a friend. "Is there something you want to start with today?"

Krystal closed her eyes before speaking. She needed a moment to get her thoughts together. All of this time she'd spent attempting to deal with her feelings related to Jerad's death and now she was back to square one. Her relationship with Antonio was significantly different from the one she'd shared with Jerad, and yet her feelings about his death were familiar.

"Krystal, if you don't want to talk about Antonio's death, we can talk about something else."

"No, I want to talk about it."

The woman waited for her to continue. When she didn't, she asked, "How do you feel about losing Antonio?"

"I miss him." She paused, opening her eyes to focus on the marble desk water fountain just past the doctor's shoulder. "A lot."

"What do you miss the most?"

"Even when I did something that I knew was wrong, he'd always be there for me. He used to give me these crazy lectures about what men wanted from women. And outside of Yohan, most of what he said I believed was true.

"I'll never forget the first time I snuck out to meet someone. I guess he spotted me creeping out of the front door. He followed me all night. Me and the guy I left with sat out in his car talking for a couple of hours before I went back to the house. Before I could get up the stairs, Tonio was standing in the walkway waiting for me." Krystal stopped. The more she thought about him the more she missed him.

"Anything else?"

"Been thinking about dying a lot too." She didn't lower her eyes this time. She stared her therapist straight in the face when she said it.

"Dying or death?"

"Dying." Krystal was very clear on what she felt now. Before, she would have confused the two, but she'd recently experienced both and she knew the difference.

"Have you thought about taking your own life?"

"I don't know." This time she did turn from the woman. "Sometimes it feels like the pill bottles are calling to me. I wonder what it's like on the other side. You know, at the funeral I swore I heard Tonio talking to me. He said it was beautiful on the other side. I can't help but to think if I'd be better off with them."

"But what about your friends? What about the people in your life right now that care about you? What about Yohan, and the man sitting out in the waiting room? What happens to them if you take your own life?"

"They're stronger than I am." The words sounded weak, but Krystal was attempting to use it as the perfect excuse to focus only on herself.

"You're stronger than this. You've made it this far. Don't you think it will hurt them if you commit suicide?"

Krystal didn't want to think about this. She just wanted it to all go away. She was tired inside. Tired of living, tired of fighting, tired of feeling like anyone she got close to would eventually die.

Krystal usually let the doctor ask all of the questions, but she had one for her today. "Why did they have to leave me?"

"Are you asking me as your therapist or as a person?"

"A person." Krystal focused on her hands, picking at a tattered cuticle.

"Then I'd have to say that death is a natural part of life. Sometimes we can anticipate it, sometimes we can't. We just have to cherish the time we have with people and remember how they've touched our lives."

"But what do you do when every time you get close to a person they die?"

"Is that what you fear?"

Krystal grabbed the tissue from the box on the end table and wiped the tears from her eyes. The earlier drizzle on the other side of the window had turned into a furious downpour, and the roaring of thunder shook the walls around them. The blood pulsing through the veins in her head forced her to massage circles on her temples to ease the pain.

"How much time do we have left?" She didn't want to talk about this. She'd thought that saying the words, getting her feelings out in the open would ease the pain in her heart. Instead, she felt worse than she had when she'd first arrived.

"We still have a few minutes."

"Can we talk about something else?"

"Sure." The woman flipped through Krystal's chart before continuing. "How's the medication working out? Are you experiencing any side effects?"

"I decided not to take it. I hate taking pills."

"I understand, but I do think the medication may help you."

"I'll think about it, but I can't guarantee that I'll use it."

"Here." The woman handed Krystal a business card.

"I want you to keep this with you at all times. If for any reason you need to talk to someone, call the number on the card. Someone is available twenty-four hours a day, seven days a week."

"I will." She twirled the card between her fingers before sliding it into her purse.

"Is there anything else you would like to talk about? You still have a few minutes."

"No."

The doctor scribbled a few additional notes into the file on her desk before standing. "I'll be back in a minute with your paperwork." She exited the room, leaving Krystal to think about what they'd talked about today.

Krystal's eyes scanned the room, taking in the shelves lined with medical books. To her surprise, the books on the highest shelf weren't medical books but rather books of poetry. She made her way over to the shelf to get a closer look. Just as she reached to pull out a volume of work by Paul Laurence Dunbar, the doctor returned. She pulled her hand back, her eyes turning toward the floor like a child just caught with her hand in the cookie jar.

"Would you like to take it?" she asked, noticing Krystal's reaction to her presence.

"May I?"

The doctor reached above her, sliding the book from between a book by Jay Wright and Zora Neale Hurston's *Every Tongue Got to Confess*. "Keep it. I hope it inspires you as much as it has me."

"Thank you."

"Here's your paperwork." She handed Krystal a pink sheet of paper along with a new prescription. "If there isn't anything else, Mr. Fedichi is in the lobby waiting for you."

"Thanks again."

"You're welcome. And don't forget; if you ever need to talk, call the number on the card."

"I will."

Krystal turned, and picking up her purse from the chair she'd been sitting in, she walked out the door to face life.

Chapter Twenty-five

Andre walked a constant path behind the couch in his living room. Thoughts of how to approach Krystal raced through his mind. He needed to find out what had happened between her and Yohan. They needed each other now more than ever. Finally, he turned and headed in the direction of her bedroom. He was getting nowhere fighting with himself, so he decided to get the information straight from the horse's mouth.

"Krystal?" He tapped on her bedroom door. "Can I come in?"

"Go away," she yelled back through the wood.

"Look, I need to know what's going on with you and Yohan." Since Krystal moved back to his house, Andre had only seen Yohan once. He'd stopped by the day after the fight to check on her and bring her roses as a peace offering. She refused to see him. He assured Yohan she just needed some time and he'd get her home as soon as possible. But that was almost a week ago.

"Leave me alone."

"Look, you haven't been home in a week and Yohan

hasn't been to work in days. Brey and I are starting to worry."

Krystal stared at the locked door, wondering for the first time if Yohan was all right. After Antonio died, Yohan jumped right in, taking over the additional responsibilities. Lately, he'd spent so much time tending to business she rarely saw him. But the night he discovered her smoking weed, something was different. She didn't even remember what he said to her, just the disappointment and hurt in his eyes.

"Krystal, open this door before I break it down!"

Hunching her shoulders and releasing an angry sigh, she climbed from the bed and unlocked the door without opening it.

Andre turned the knob and pushed as he entered the room. He watched her for a moment as she stared out into the sunset. The past week she'd spent doing the same thing: school, cheerleading practice, therapy, and ending her day hiding behind a closed and locked door.

Andre worried about her. But moreso he worried about her treatment of Yohan. They'd never fought like this. Krystal was being especially cruel to him, avoiding any and all contact. The last time he spoke to Yohan, he saw through the wall erected around his emotions. Though he tried to hide it, Andre clearly saw that being away from Krystal was tearing him up inside.

"Krystal?"

"What? Come in here to take his side?"

"Actually, I don't know either side. Yohan basically told me if you wanted me to know what was going on you'd tell me yourself. Whether you believe it or not, his loyalty lies with you." He slid the chair from beneath the computer desk and straddled it.

She faced him, not believing the words he'd just spoken. She was sure Yohan had told them he'd caught her smoking weed. "He didn't say anything?" she asked in confusion.

"Not a word. He also hasn't come out of that apartment in three days."

"Are you sure?" Again she turned her back on him, her gaze focused on the sun slipping beneath the top of the trees lining the end of the parking lot. "Maybe he went out while you took care of your business."

"Come on, Krystal, if he hasn't been to work, he hasn't been anywhere. Now tell me what's going on."

"I don't want to talk about it."

"Is that the line you fed him? You know that shit's not going to fly with me. You're not being fair to him."

"Fair? Oh, so you wanna talk about fair? What about being fair to me? Huh?" Krystal's voice escalated as she spoke. "Since Tonio died, he spends all of his time with you. Yeah, he gets up in the morning and takes me to school. He's there to pick me up after cheerleading practice, but other than that I barely see him. He doesn't even take me to therapy anymore."

She sounded so spoiled, and Andre blamed himself for it. Since they brought her to Lincoln Heights, they'd basically done to her what Jerad's father had done to him. Instead of addressing issues as they arose, they gave her all of the attention in the world. Now their world had changed. Yohan had significantly more responsibilities and some big shoes to fill.

Unlike the rest of them, Yohan didn't have time to mourn. If he wasn't out handling business, he was trying to hold his home together and worrying about Krystal. Andre and Aubrey agreed Yohan was spending a good amount of time with them, but they'd attributed it to him using work as a way to deal with Antonio's death. Now,

Andre wondered if there was more to it, that maybe Yohan was trying to hold it together for Krystal, afraid if he stopped, he'd break down.

"I need to tell you something," he said in a solemn but serious tone.

"Here it comes, the 'you should think of others' lecture."

"I'm not going to lecture you. Now, are you going to let me tell you what you need to know?"

"Go ahead." Smacking her lips, she plopped down on the bed, rolled her eyes, and crossed her arms over her chest. She'd allow him to tell his story. It wasn't going to change anything, though. What mattered was she needed Yohan now and he wasn't there for her.

"A couple of years before you came to us, I got a call from the manager of the garage about an abandoned Cutlass parked behind the shop. We didn't think anything of it. We figured it was stolen and some kids probably just dumped it behind the building before the cops caught up to them."

"Where are you going with this?"

"Patience. I'm getting there. Like I was saying, when Tonio and I got down there with the towing company, we realized the car wasn't abandoned. Man, the look on Yohan's face when he woke to the barrel of Antonio's forty-five Magnum was priceless. Wished I'd had a camera, 'cause that was surely a Kodak moment.

"Anyway, Antonio got him to roll down the window. Yohan told us he'd just gotten to Atlanta and he didn't have any place to go. He'd been staying in hotels until his money ran out and he'd been living out of his car since. Tonio believed young buck's story, so he offered Yohan a job at the shop and a place to stay."

"What else did he tell you?" Krystal was curious. She'd always assumed Yohan was raised in Lincoln

Heights and that's how he came to be so close to The Trio. She had no idea they'd just stumbled upon him and took him in.

"I don't know much else about Yohan's past—only that his pops left him and his moms when he was real young. His moms raised him until he just up and left home one day. He still sends her money once a week. He was a sixteen-year-old boy with no direction when he came here. I taught him how to treat a woman, Brey taught him how to keep a family together, and Tonio taught him everything else about being a man."

"I didn't know," Krystal replied after taking a moment to digest the information he'd just relayed to her.

"There's more. Did you take the time to realize Yohan hasn't stopped since Tonio died?" When she didn't respond, he continued. "You know, Brey and I were emotional wrecks when we left the hospital. We just couldn't deal. If it hadn't have been for Yohan handling the funeral arrangements, I don't know what would have happened. We didn't have to do anything but show up."

"How come he didn't say anything?"

"He's a man, Krystal. We don't talk about this kind of shit the way women do. He's still running on adrenaline and when he crashes, he's going to need you by his side. He hasn't mourned and he needs to, but he can't because he's worried about you."

The realization weighed heavily on Krystal's heart. She'd been so absorbed in her problems she hadn't taken the time to see Yohan was hurting. She'd probably made things worse by just cutting him out of her life. He gave her everything, loved her unconditionally, and this is how she repaid him. She needed to make things right and she needed to do it now.

"Guess I'd better go home."

"You know my door is always open. If either of you

need to talk, you know where to find me." He got up from the chair, prepared to let her go home.

She moved across the room to hug one of the three remaining men in her life. "You still gave me a lecture,"— She pulled out of his embrace and smiled up at him—"but I needed one. Guess I've been acting like a spoiled brat."

"Your words. Not mine."

"If you say so." Krystal grabbed the sweatshirt draped over the chair and slid it on. "I'd better get home to check on my man."

"Yeah. You do that. And Krystal, one more thing." Dre stopped her before she reached the door.

"Yeah?"

He narrowed his eyes, insuring she clearly understood the seriousness of what he was about to say. His entire demeanor changed as his posture straightened and he glared at her. "Don't you ever again come into my house smelling like weed. You understand me?"

Krystal lowered her eyes and in a soft tone replied, "Yes." She then turned and made her way out the door.

Dre watched as she walked away. She'd been through so much in her life and he hated that all of this had happened to her. He glanced around the room at the cheery lilac walls and framed pictures of flowers in bloom and children playing, and he had to wonder if Krystal had ever enjoyed the carefree life of just being a child. She'd been touched by so many adult issues at such a young age, he wondered if she'd ever truly adjust to living life without fear of losing those she cherished most.

He turned, prepared to exit the room when a folded piece of paper on the floor next to her desk caught his eye. He scooped up the yellow piece of stationery. For a moment, he thought about not reading it. He normally respected Krystal's privacy, but with all that had been going on the need to know the words on the page took precedence over her privacy.

He opened the note and began to read. The words on the page pained him to his heart and caused a sense of failure to wash over him.

Sometimes I just wish it would all be over. Maybe I'd be better off with Jerad and Antonio. I don't know how to deal with this. I'm so confused. Why is all of this happening to me? Why is it that whenever I get close to someone they're snatched away in the blink of an eye? I'm afraid. I guess it's a good thing that Yohan and I aren't speaking. Maybe if I stay away he won't leave me either.

That pill bottle is calling my name again. Maybe I should have done it in the first place. But what if it didn't work? What if it just made things worse? What if I was stuck here like a vegetable and the guys had to take care of me? What am I thinking? I just don't know how much longer I can do this.

Her rambling on the page stopped there. Dre sat on the bed, head tilted back, fighting off the many emotions vying for escape. He didn't know how to help her. Right now he didn't really know how to help himself. So he did the only thing he could think to do. Pray.

Chapter Twenty-six

Krystal expected to find Yohan sitting at the television playing Xbox like he usually did when he was stressed. Instead she found the apartment devoid of light and reeking of dirty dishes and alcohol. Since the place was dark, she assumed he was in the bedroom. She didn't bother to turn on the lights. She'd arranged the furniture so that lights weren't necessary to venture from the front door to the bedrooms.

Turning on the light in the master bath, she expected Yohan to be stretched across the bed, passed out. But he wasn't there. She checked the spare bedroom, thinking he'd been too drunk to tell them apart, but he wasn't there, either. She was sure he hadn't left; his truck was still parked out front.

Making her way back to the living room, the sound of a bottle sliding across the hardwood floors startled her. Flipping on the lamp, she found him lying on his back, one arm laid across his forehead, the other hanging off of the side of the sofa with an empty bottle of Hennessy loosely in his grip. The light must have momentarily jarred him from his sleep because he dropped the bottle and buried his head in the cushions.

Krystal looked around at the mountain of empty Hennessy and Heineken bottles, every clue indicating Yohan had spent the last three days cooped up in the apartment attempting to drink his troubles away. Andre was right. When he finally stopped, he'd had to face the fact that Antonio was dead. She should have been here for him just like he'd always been there for her. She blamed herself for his current situation and she promised, somehow, some way, she'd make it up to him.

She picked up the phone and dialed Andre's number.

"Yeah?"

"Can you come down here? I need to get Yohan in the bed."

"What's wrong?" Dre grabbed his keys and headed for the door.

"He's going to have one hell of a hangover. He'll be fine once he sobers up."

"Be there in a minute." Dre took a moment to calm his nerves. He still held the note in his hands. He rubbed his fingers over the handwritten words, contemplating what to say to Krystal. They needed to talk about this. He didn't want to slip back into their old pattern of showering her with attention as if everything was just fine. Things weren't fine. The words on the page clearly indicated that much.

Folding the paper and sliding it into his back pocket, Dre decided he'd take care of the Yohan situation first and then sit down and have a talk with Krystal. He was prepared for her anger at him for snooping through her personal belongings, but in the end, hopefully she'd understand why he did it.

Krystal stood in the doorway of the apartment waiting for him.

"Where is he?" Dre asked, stepping into the still dark apartment.

"On the couch. Just take him back to the bedroom."

Dre scooped Yohan from the couch and headed down the hallway toward the master bedroom. Once out of Krystal's sight, Andre shook his head as he laid Yohan in the bed. If he hadn't left the bottles of Hennessy in the house, Yohan probably wouldn't have drunk so much. Closing the bedroom door, he found Krystal in the kitchen washing the dishes she'd left in the sink almost a week ago. It appeared Yohan hadn't done anything but drink since she left.

"Don't even say it," she said, not giving Andre the chance to fix his mouth to say *I told you so.*

"What? I wasn't going to say anything." Dre tried to sound innocent, but failed terribly.

"Yeah right, and the Irish don't drink green beer on St. Patrick's Day."

"Ha ha." He stepped up next to her. Grabbing a dish towel, he proceeded to pick up the glasses she'd just washed and dried them off.

Krystal cut her eye at him. She'd never seen him do a lick of housework, not even when she lived in his place. His girl always did the dishes and vacuumed and any other housework that needed to be done. In turn, he took care of the things she thought should be done by her man.

Curiosity getting the best of her, Krystal said, "Spill it."

"Spill what?"

"You don't do housework, so start talking."

Dre huffed before placing the glass on the counter. He placed his palms on the countertop, dropping his head. Thoughts of what to say to her raced through his mind. He reached into his pocket, pulling out the folded piece of yellow stationery. "I found this in your room."

Krystal's eyes turned down to glimpse the bright yellow piece of paper. She crossed her arms, glaring at him. "You went through my stuff?"

"No. You dropped it when you left."

Snatching the paper from his hands, she yelled, "That didn't give you the right to read it."

"But I did and I can't go back and change it." Dre tried to remain calm. All he wanted to do was reach out and hold her in his arms. He wanted to comfort her, protect her, and assure her that everything would be fine. But the truth of the matter was, he wasn't sure himself if everything would turn out for the best.

"Look, Krystal, I don't want things to go back to how they were. You and I both know that shit wasn't healthy. I want you to be able to talk to me, or Brey or Yohan. You can't keep holding things inside."

"And what if I want to? What if it's the only way I know how to cope?" She turned from him, fighting back tears. She wasn't ready for them to know what she was feeling. She'd barely been able to talk about it in therapy. Krystal found that writing things down helped, but she wasn't ready to share her feelings and now Dre knew. Losing the battle with the tears, her hand grasped at the counter before her legs gave way.

Dre wrapped his arms around her, pulling her into a loving embrace. He couldn't allow her to continue like this. He needed to find a way to get through to her, make her understand that the longer she held things in, the worse the consequences when they finally did surface.

No longer able to think about it anymore, he carried her over to the couch. He held her in his arms, rocking her gently until she succumbed to sleep. Carrying her to the spare bedroom, he laid her in the bed to get some much needed rest. Dre looked in on Yohan before quietly creeping out of the front door. He'd figure something out, but right now Krystal and Yohan needed to get their rest.

Chapter Twenty-seven

Since climbing out of the bed in the middle of the night, Krystal found herself in the same spot Yohan occupied the day after her breakdown. For once, she saw things through his eyes. He'd been out for nearly twelve hours. She only left his bedside twice, once to go to the bathroom and once to grab something to eat.

Andre and Aubrey stopped by a couple of times just to make sure everything was copacetic. She assured them she'd take good care of Yohan and she'd let them know as soon as he was well enough to return to work.

Yohan stirred beneath the quilt she'd tossed over him. His face turning up in a frown, he draped his arm over his eyes in a desperate attempt to block out the blinding sun. As the blinds closed, he realized he wasn't alone.

"Need me to get you anything?" Krystal asked.

Yohan squinted at the shadowy figure moving across the room. Even with the blinds closed, the light seeping in appeared too bright. He quickly released the gesture as the throbbing in his head intensified. "A new head and a breath mint would be good."

Krystal smiled at him. Even hungover, he tried to keep his sense of humor. "I can't help you with the new head, but we do have some aspirin."

Yohan leaned up in bed a little too fast and the room spun. He fought back the bile rising in his throat.

"There's a bucket by the bed if you need it," Krystal pointed out before leaving the bedroom. She didn't mind cleaning up his vomit. He'd done it for her when she'd gotten food poisoning and those rare months when Mother Nature decided to be especially cruel to her during her cycle. Maybe she'd get the chance to return the favor.

"Here." She handed him two aspirin and a glass of water. She then poured fresh coffee from the pot into a mug for him. They kept coffee in the house for times like this, though Andre was usually the one hungover.

Yohan was never much of a hard liquor drinker. True, he drank the occasional shot of scotch, but other than that, he preferred malt liquor and beer. The only reason the bottles of Hennessy lined the shelves of the liquor cabinet was because Andre left them the last time they'd had a poker night at the apartment.

Krystal watched Yohan drain the last of the coffee from the cup. He leaned his head back, resting it against the headboard, attempting to will away the little drummer beating against his skull.

"Yohan, I am so sorry," Krystal said, lowering her eyes in shame.

"Don't be. I should have just faced his death."

"I should have been here for you instead of acting like a brat. You've always been there for me, and I should have seen that you were going through something, but I was too caught up in what I thought I was missing."

"You have your own demons to deal with." He didn't want her blaming herself for what happened. He knew sooner or later he'd need to deal with it. A part of him wished she'd been there for him, but the other part was relieved she didn't have to watch a grown man cry.

"Come here." He opened his arms to her and she slid in the bed between his legs. It felt good to have her in his arms again. She'd been out of his life for a week and it had been the worst week of his life. But she was back now and hopefully they'd be able to salvage their tattered relationship.

"I love you, Yohan," Krystal confessed as she shifted in his arms to get more comfortable.

"I love you too, baby. I love you too."

Chapter Twenty-eight

Two weeks after she'd returned to the home where she belonged, Krystal picked up her two-way to send a message to Octavio. She hadn't heard from him in nearly three weeks. She only sent the message to say hello. The last time they'd spoken, he said he was headed out of town and he'd be back in a couple of weeks. She didn't mind their time apart. She'd spent most of the time dealing with Antonio's death and trying to get her life back on track.

HOW ARE YOU? His message read.

I'M MAKING IT. STILL JUST TAKING IT DAY BY DAY.

SORRY ABOUT YOUR BROTHER. DID THEY FIND OUT WHAT HAPPENED?

CAN WE TALK IN PERSON? she typed back.

SURE. WANT ME TO COME GET YOU?

NO. MEET ME . . . Krystal typed in a location and a time for him to meet her. Yohan was working at the club tonight with Aubrey, so she had plenty of time. Besides, Octavio was just a friend and she saw nothing wrong with meeting up with a friend.

*   *   *

Krystal sat in a restaurant with her back to the door. She didn't know why, but for some reason she just didn't want to see Octavio approach. Things were different now. For the first time in a long time, she was sure of one thing, and that was she loved Yohan. Though Octavio was only a friend, she felt the need to sever the few ties they shared. She didn't want him paging her anymore. She'd been lucky thus far that Yohan hadn't suspected anything was going on between them.

Krystal was also concerned that Octavio didn't fear Yohan or The Trio. Sometimes she wondered what was going through that mind of his. He didn't seem the least bit fazed the night at the club when they'd been caught together. She wondered if he really thought them capable of killing him.

"What's on your mind?" Octavio asked as he slipped into the seat beside her.

"You."

"Really? Do tell."

She looked around at the prying eyes surrounding them. Having second thoughts, she asked, "Is there somewhere we can go? You know, a little more private?"

"How about my place? That's only if you feel comfortable being there with me."

Krystal thought about it for a second. She wasn't afraid he was going to do anything to her. He'd only been respectful since the first time they'd met. "Okay."

The trip to the Residence Inn where he was staying only took fifteen minutes. They'd spent the short trip catching up on the few things that had transpired in their lives since the last time they talked.

"After you." Octavio pushed the door open and allowed her to precede him into the room.

The furniture was standard for a hotel room. The only

difference was the place was a little more spacious than a one-night stay at a hotel room. Besides the couch, table, and chairs, it had a full kitchen with a refrigerator, sink, stove, and cabinets.

"Would you like something to drink?"

"Sure. What do you have?"

As Octavio rambled through the refrigerator and cabinets, Krystal took a seat on the couch. She grabbed a magazine from the table and flipped through the pages.

"I have bottled water, soda, and orange juice."

"Bottled water is fine." Reading through an article in *Sports Illustrated*, Krystal glanced over the top of the magazine. She noticed a manila folder peeking out from under another magazine stacked on the table. She still heard Octavio in the kitchen behind her, so she took the time to slide the magazine over just enough to get a good look at the name written in red ink across the top.

"You want a glass?" he asked before exiting the kitchen.

She dropped the magazine in her hand on top of the other one before he realized she'd seen the file.

"No. The bottle's fine." She sat stunned at what she'd just read.

"Here you go."

She wrapped her fingers around the bottle, quickly unscrewing the top and guzzling down the liquid. She closed her eyes, savoring the wetness sliding down her throat, quenching the sudden dryness. She needed to see what was in that file, but first, she needed to figure out a way to get Octavio out of the room. Looking around, she realized she'd left her purse in the truck.

"I left my purse in the car. You mind getting it for me?"

"Sure. Make yourself at home."

She grabbed the file again as Octavio slipped out of sight. Reading the pages, Krystal didn't know what to think. The folder contained page after page of locations, dates, times, and maps. Each page documented Yohan's whereabouts most hours of the day. The further into the file she delved, the more information about her appeared. Not only had Octavio been watching Yohan, he'd been following her.

She turned to the last page and read the handwritten notes.

Bounty for the return of Yohannes Doran Hampton, five hundred thousand dollars. Last seen in a red Cutlass with Virginia plates. Possibly in the Atlanta, GA area.

The sound of Octavio's voice coming closer startled her. She assumed by the broken conversation he was on the phone. She quickly replaced the file beneath the pile of magazines and stood, trying her best to look inconspicuous.

"Here you—"

"Take me home." Krystal cut him off. She stared at him, anger blazing in her eyes. It was taking everything in her not to say anything about what she'd just read. She needed some time to process the information before she said anything to him.

"What's wrong?"

"Look, just take me home."

"Okay," he replied.

She stormed past him, heading straight for his truck, not taking the time to grab her purse. When she reached the parking lot, she stopped two steps from the curb. He hadn't yet caught up with her, so she had a few moments to take in the sight.

Krystal inched closer to the damaged passenger side quarter panel of his Durango. She ran her hand over the pearl white paint he hadn't been able to wash off. Jerking her hand away, everything went blurry. Her body swayed and she reached for the hood to steady herself. She crossed one arm over her stomach, covered her forehead and eyes with the other, and doubled over at her body's urge to rid itself of anything she may have eaten in the past hour. No matter how much she tried, it just kept coming. Finally she stopped fighting and allowed her body to relax and expel the food naturally.

Her stomach now empty of the nourishment she'd consumed earlier, Krystal rested her arms and forehead against the door. She concentrated on her breathing and holding down the acid now filling her empty stomach. Her body jumped as Octavio placed his hand firmly against her back.

"You all right?"

"I don't feel too well. I need to get home."

He helped her into the vehicle and fulfilled her request. He too would feel better once she was home.

After a long, hot bath, Krystal crawled in the bed. The warmth of the covers comforted her. She'd thought about what she'd discovered and she'd already begun to plot her revenge. When the realization that Octavio had been using her all along had finally hit her, it wasn't a pretty picture. Now, she just needed to be sure. She needed to hear herself say the words before Octavio's fate would be set in stone. She picked up the phone and called the one person she knew would listen objectively and possibly give her good advice.

As she waited for China to answer, Krystal thought back to the night she'd had the dream about Yohan's truck being run off of the road. The more she thought about it, the angrier she got. Her lips twisted into the most unpleasant face. Her ears burned as the rage took refuge in her blood. Her hand throbbed as she squeezed down hard on the cordless phone.

"Hey, Krystal," China answered.

"I need to talk to you about some fucked-up shit."

"What's up?"

Krystal thought for a moment about what she wanted to say. Did she really want to pull China into this? Things had gotten out of hand with Octavio and now she knew the truth.

"Krystal! Krystal!"

"Yeah. Aye, remember when I told you about Octavio?"

"Yeah. I also remember warning you that he was trouble. Now spill it."

Krystal took in a deep breath and with a huff, forced it out. She knew she was about to get the *I told you so* speech and she was so not in the mood for that. A moment more of contemplation and she said the words, "He killed Antonio."

"You lying," China replied with disbelief.

"I wish." Krystal still couldn't believe how naive she'd been. China had tried to warn her that Octavio was up to no good, but she just wouldn't listen. Now Antonio was dead and her so-called friend was the person responsible.

"Krystal, I am so sorry."

"Not as sorry as his ass is gonna be."

China detected the anger in Krystal's voice and it worried her. They'd both been around Lincoln Heights long enough to know how things worked. If Krystal bought into the philosophy that the members of the LHC took care of their own, then she knew exactly what her girl was thinking. "Listen to me, Krystal. You need to tell Yohan about this."

"Oh, hell naw. This muthafucka gonna pay. And I'm takin' his ass out myself."

"Come on, Krystal. Think about what you're saying. You're not going to kill anyone."

"The hell I ain't. He crossed the line, China. I can't just walk away from this."

"And how exactly do you plan on pulling this off?" China needed to convince Krystal what she was thinking was a bad idea. She was sure she hadn't thought through this, so she was convinced she could still talk her out of it.

"Don't worry about those details. I've got someone who owes me big. Yeah, I'll take care of Octavio's ass." Krystal didn't hear the next question. She basically tuned China out as all of the pieces of her plan laid themselves out before her.

"Look, I gotta go," Krystal said as she figured out the last piece of her plan.

"Krystal? Have you heard a word I've said?"

"It doesn't matter. What's done is done. I'm gonna take care of this my way."

"You know I'ma have to tell Yohan."

"You wouldn't dare."

"Try me," China said, making it clear that she wasn't playing.

Krystal remained quiet for a moment. China was a woman of her word; still Krystal knew what their friendship meant to her, and immediately she decided to call China's bluff.

"A real friend wouldn't do that shit." She didn't give China the opportunity to respond. She hit the off button on the phone and turned off the ringer. If China wanted to tell Yohan, she'd have to risk their friendship to do it.

Chapter Twenty-nine

Knocking twice, pausing and knocking three times more, Krystal waited patiently for someone to open the apartment door. She pulled the collar of her jacket up close over her ears to fight off the slight chill in the air. Though the calendar indicated spring's official arrival, the lack of sunlight led the way for a crisp coolness to creep into the darkness.

A young man no more than sixteen pulled the door open just enough for Krystal to make out his mocha complexion against the soft glow from the apartment.

"Can I help you?" he asked.

"Don't play stupid. I need to speak with Ice." She glowered at him.

"Sorry, ma'am, Ice is not taking visitors."

"Don't *ma'am* me. You know damn well who I am and believe me, he'll see me. Now go tell him who's at the door." She crossed her arms over her chest.

"And what if I don't?"

"Well then,"—She turned her eyes from the young man to examine her nails—"I'll be forced to inform my boyfriend about what's going on out of this apartment." Looking up from her hand, she again crossed her arms and glared at him, insuring he understood she wasn't here to play games.

He looked her over one good time before speaking.

"Give me a minute." He closed the door, leaving her again standing out in the night.

Krystal waited in silence, listening to the purr of engines coming and going from the entrance of the complex. Though set off to one side, this building sat perched between the leasing office and the man-made pond near the metal gate guarding the entryway. The sound of the chain beating against the door as someone slid it from the latch drew her attention from the sights and sounds of the night.

A different pair of eyes stared at her this time. She didn't recognize the harsh facial features of the brown-skinned gentleman. He scrutinized her every move with a nerve-wrenching glare. Krystal refused to allow his inspection to deter her from the task at hand. True, he looked as if he could do some serious damage, but she doubted he'd consider doing more than escorting her through the tiny apartment Ice conducted his business from.

"After you."

The husky voice caught her by surprise. It reminded her of one of the old men in the movies who'd spent most of his life smoking to the point where his vocal cords were reduced to no more than a stringy black mass.

The inside of the apartment contained the bare minimum: a couch, big-screen television, gaming console, and surround sound system remained the focal point of the main living area. Definitely a bachelor pad, the place contained no pictures, rugs, plants, or any indication of a woman's touch. They stopped in front of a closed door to what Krystal assumed was a bedroom turned office. Her escort knocked twice and then opened the door. Nudging her into the room, the man closed the door behind them.

"Ah, Miss Bao. Please have a seat."

Krystal sat down in the plush leather chair across the desk from Ice. Far from comfortable, she tried her best to ignore the looming presence of his goons at her back. She didn't like feeling cornered and right now her body fought her mind's beckoning to run.

"And to what do I owe this untimely visit from you?"

"You have something that I need," she replied.

"Well,"—Ice paused for a moment to take in the young woman sitting across from him—"as we discussed before, the first one is on the house. You'll have to pay for this one."

"I'm not talking about weed." She regained her confidence the moment the conversation shifted to business.

Ice raised an eyebrow at her reply. He looked at her curiously, his brow furrowing in confusion. She seemed at ease in his presence, which he found unnerving and yet intriguing. Very few people were comfortable around a known killer. He'd done his dirt to take care of business, but the police had never been able to pin anything on him. Drumming his fingers together he leaned forward. "If you're not here for my product, then there's nothing I can help you with."

"*Au contraire.* I know for a fact that you can get me what I need."

"And how is that?" He leaned back into his chair, waiting for her explanation.

"You know, you're lucky no one has slipped up. If word got back to my beau or his comrades about your business, there'd be hell to pay. Word travels fast around these parts, and you've got some loose lips for customers." She gave him a devilish smile.

She'd mastered the art of bluffing. For years she studied Aubrey during The Trio's poker games. The skill came naturally to her and by studying him, she perfected the technique. Ice didn't have what it took to bluff her. She'd been around the streets long enough to know how the game worked. He'd give her what she wanted. His business, in its current state, was too profitable for him not to.

"Leave us," he said to the two men standing at her back. Krystal watched them in the mirror hung on the wall behind Ice. The men looked at each other, then back at their boss before exiting the room.

"Now that we're alone—"

Krystal cut him off before he could complete his thought. "Look, I have some business I need to take care of. I need something compact, powerful, but quiet."

"And what exactly are you going to use this for?"

"You don't need to know all of that."

Ice took a moment to process her request.

Krystal watched his expression as he sorted out his options. His expression told her he wasn't sure he wanted to be involved in whatever it was she had in mind. But she knew if word got out, his business would be ruined. On the other hand, if he helped her, he might get pulled into something even worse. Rebuilding his business would be costly but it was possible; however, being tied to a murder he didn't commit himself was a different story.

"So what do I get out of this?" he asked before making his final decision.

"Always the businessman. You get my word that I'll handle my business quietly. You won't get any surprise visitors coming around asking questions."

"Getting pulled into your drama is the least of my concerns." He crossed his arms, cocking his head to one side with his eyebrows raised.

"Well, how about I sweeten the deal?"

"I'm listening."

"Not only will I guarantee you won't get pulled into any drama, but I'll personally see to it that what is going on here is kept quiet. I'll let you know who's in the streets singing like canaries so you can take care of things on your end. We'll call this even. And ultimately, if you help me out with this, you won't have to worry about me ever knocking on your door again asking for favors." Krystal hoped he'd bite. All she had to deal with at the moment was her word.

Without an additional moment of hesitation, he replied, "I can have what you need tomorrow night if that's doable for you. Meet me in the park at sunset."

"Can we make it a little later? My other half might still be making rounds at that time."

Ice grabbed a piece of paper and tore off a corner. He scribbled a barely legible number on it and handed it to her.

"When you're ready, call that number." He stood and made his way around the desk. Sitting on the corner, he leaned in so close Krystal could smell the alcohol on his breath. "Is there anything else I can do for the beautiful young lady?"

She watched the lust dance behind his eyes. For a moment she had second thoughts about asking him to help her, but she quickly dismissed them.

"You can escort me to the door," she replied, flashing him her pearly whites.

Standing, he offered her his arm. All eyes turned in their direction as the door swung open and they stepped into the hallway. They walked past the two gentlemen he'd excused earlier and made their way to the door. Before reaching to open it for her, he turned.

"Can I ask you something?" he said in a seductive voice.

Seeing him for the first time in full light, Krystal realized Ice was a fairly attractive guy. His features remained soft though the creases around his mouth and forehead showed his age. The layers of diamond jewelry hanging from his neck and adorning his wrists and hands told the story of why the name *Ice* stuck.

"Sure, but that doesn't mean I'm going to give you an answer."

"Call me curious, but why are you doing this? I mean, I'm sure any business you may have could be handled by your man or your family."

"Let's just say this is personal. I can handle my business. I think the real question here is can you handle yours?"

She reached for the door handle, giving him a seductive look. He stopped her hand just before it reached the knob. Turning it and opening the door for her, he replied, "Maybe one day, if you give me a chance, I'll show you how well I can handle business."

Krystal stepped into the night without responding to his pass at her. She knew how to use what she had to get what she wanted. She also knew if Yohan ever found out about any of this, Ice wouldn't live to see another day.

Chapter Thirty

The brisk wind rubbed Krystal's exposed face as she stood in the park waiting for Ice to show. A light mist coated her skin, cooling the burning beneath her cheeks and eyes. She allowed only one tear to fall. It would be the last she'd shed for her dearly departed Antonio.

Her plan played over and over again in her mind. She'd surprise Octavio with a bottle of wine, drug him, tie him up, and end this all. She'd had Dre's woman sew in a weave to make sure she didn't leave any hair in his hotel room. Her silk gloves covered her from fingers to elbows. She carried a bag just large enough to conceal the bottle of wine and two glasses. She planned to take the evidence with her. She'd tuck the gun into the inside pocket of the quarter-length coat she wore.

"You look to have a lot on your mind."

Krystal glanced over her shoulder to see Ice approaching from behind. "Did you bring me what I need?" She didn't turn to face him. Instead her gaze remained fixated on the sky above as she fought back tears.

"I could get into a lot of trouble for this." Ice stopped a few steps behind her.

"Having a change of heart?"

"Not at all. I'd just hate for something to go wrong and such a beautiful young woman end up ruining her life."

Truth be told, Ice was having second thoughts about her doing this, or at least her doing it alone. If he helped her, he could hold this over her, maybe work his way into the good graces of The Trio and make his life much easier.

"You don't know anything about my life."

"True, but I know you have potential. You need to let whatever this is go."

"That's not an option." Her voice stayed calm, steady, and it almost scared her.

"Then at least allow me to help."

"Can't." That was just it. Even if she wanted help, Krystal had to do this on her own. She was partially responsible for Antonio's death, but she'd be completely responsible for avenging it.

"Why not?"

"Like I told you before, this is personal."

"Revenge always is." He closed the distance between them so that they stood side by side. He handed her the package wrapped in a dark-colored cloth.

She took the gift, unwrapping the pistol and the silencer. After a quick examination, she folded the ends of the cloth back over the weapon, protecting it from the elements. She slid it into her jacket pocket without saying a word.

"The silencer screws on," he added. "You sure there's nothing else I can do for you?" He reached over to her, wiping away the teardrop sliding down her cheek.

"Can you give me a lift?"

"Sure. Come on."

Krystal remained two steps behind him as they walked

toward the parking lot to where his Navigator waited. When he opened the door, she expected one of his boys to be lounging in the backseat. To her surprise, he was alone. He helped her into the truck and once she was situated, he closed the door. Climbing into the driver's seat, he asked, "So where to?"

Krystal gave him some general directions. She had him drop her off a few blocks from the hotel Octavio was staying in. With Ice's help, Krystal climbed out of the vehicle.

"I guess this is where we part ways." Staring down into her eyes, he wanted to do more than he already had. She appeared to be troubled. He even considered pulling this job off for her just to no longer see the pain she harbored.

"Thanks again."

"You're welcome. I hope things go well for you."

"So do I." The awkward silence becoming uncomfortable, she turned from him and walked toward the main street.

Climbing back in the truck, Ice watched her round the corner. He considered following her for a second, then decided the less he knew the better.

The metal door to Octavio's room was no different from the other Residence Inn doors lining either side of the manicured walkway. She stared at the numbers on the door contemplating her next move. She'd come this far and before the night was over, only one person would leave this place alive.

Plastering a convincingly fake smile across her face, Krystal knocked and waited. It only took a second for Octavio to swing the front door open.

"Krystal? What are you doing here?"

"I was just in the neighborhood and decided to stop by." She slipped past him into the well-lit room, not giving him time to invite her in. "I hope you don't mind." She lowered her chin, batting innocent eyelashes at him. Yohan always called her an actress, and tonight she was putting it on thick.

Octavio looked around outside one last time, making sure no prying eyes saw the young woman sashay her way into his humble abode. When he was sure the coast was clear, he closed the door and joined Krystal on the couch. He glanced over her outfit, taking notice of the skintight leather pants and the V cut of her halter top.

"So to what do I owe this visit from you?"

"Just needed to get out. Yohan has been on my ass twenty-four-seven since that night at the club." She relaxed, giving him a convincing grin.

"So where is he now?"

"Work as usual. I have a few hours before I have to check in, so I decided to spread my wings for a little while. Look." She pulled the bottle of wine and two glasses from her bag. "I even brought refreshments." Quickly getting up from the sofa, she made her way into the kitchen. "You got a corkscrew in here somewhere?" she asked, rambling through the nearly empty kitchen drawers.

"Third drawer to the left of the sink."

"Got it." Krystal proceeded to fill the two glasses, making sure to keep her back turned to Octavio. She then opened the small vile of clear liquid and poured half of it into one of the drinks.

"Here you go." She plopped down in the chair across from him, taking a gulp from the dark liquid in her glass.

Octavio swirled the liquid around, taking a whiff of the aroma before taking his first taste. "Aren't you a little young to be drinking?"

"Hey, a little wine never hurt anyone."

"Still,"—The last of the liquid slid down his throat, quenching his thirst—"you're underage."

"Well, I'm underage for a lot of things." Krystal inched out of the chair and straddled Octavio on the couch. She leaned over so he had a perfect view of her breasts as she placed her half-empty glass on the table behind him. "But it's never stopped me from going after what I wanted."

Krystal released a soft moan as Octavio ran his tongue between her cleavage, sliding his lips around one breast and sucking. She wrapped her hands around his ears, pulling his head back from the place where he'd made himself comfortable. She looked down into his eyes and watched as the drug glazed them over.

"Let's take this to the bedroom." She slid her hands down between his legs, feeling how much his body wanted to share itself with her.

As soon as Octavio lay down on the bed, the room spun. Everything around him danced in a light haze until it all eventually succumbed to darkness.

Octavio struggled to open his eyes. It took him a moment to get oriented. The comfort of the bed reassured him that he was still at the temporary home he'd been in for the past six weeks. He attempted to lean up, but soon discovered that his hands were tied above him. Trying desperately to move his legs, he realized that they too were immobilized. The room around him was dimly lit and movement to his right caught his attention.

"Krystal?"

The petite figure staring out of the window ignored the summons from the bed.

"Krystal, is that you?" He strained to get a look at the figure. He was sure it was her, but he wondered why she refused to answer him. "What did you do to me? And why am I tied to the bed?"

Finally, Krystal turned to face him and for the first time, Octavio saw the lines of mascara streaked down her cheeks. Even across the partially lit room he could clearly see the anger replacing any sadness in her eyes. Then, everything else about her changed. Her demeanor became rigid, serious. In the short time he'd been following her, Octavio had never seen her like this.

"It was you all along," she finally said, her voice holding confidence and anger.

"I don't know what you're talking about."

"Cut the bullshit. You know exactly what the fuck I'm talking about. I know why you're here, but most of all, I know what you did."

"Look, Krystal, whatever you think I did—"

"Stop it. Stop fucking playing games." She grabbed the lamp from the nightstand and flung it across the room. "Now, I'm going to give you one chance to explain away the white paint on your truck." She waited, nearly snarling as Octavio contemplated how to get out of his current predicament. When it became apparent he didn't have an answer, she continued, "You killed my brother and now I'm going to kill you."

"It was as accident, Krystal. I swear."

"It was an accident, all right; an accident that Antonio was driving instead of Yohan. Either way, the results remain the same. You left him out there to die and now it's your turn."

Octavio struggled to loosen the ropes.

"I wouldn't advise doing that. Just like a Chinese finger trap, the more you fight, the tighter the knots get."

The sound of the clip locking into place drew Octavio's attention away from the ropes and toward Krystal. He hadn't seen the weapon earlier. He watched with uneasiness as she screwed the silencer onto the barrel of the weapon. Beads of sweat formed on his forehead and tears filled his eyes as the reality of his situation sank in.

"Please, Krystal, don't do this."

"And why shouldn't I? Why should you get to live when Antonio didn't?" Her voice escalated as the anger poured out of her.

"Think about what you're about to do. You don't really want to do this."

"Oh, I've thought about this. I've had plenty of time to think about what I'd do to the person who took Antonio away. But I never imagined it was you."

"You have to believe me. I never meant for anyone to die," he pleaded.

"Then why'd you run? After what you did, how could you just leave him in that ditch to die?" Krystal paced between the wall and the bed. She waved the gun in his face with each and every word she spoke. She was far from losing her nerve, but she needed answers.

"I don't know. The whole time I was following him, I was thinking 'what am I doing?' Then he slowed. I guess he realized I was tailing him. For the first time in my life I freaked. All I could see was your face staring at me. He must have stopped while I was daydreaming. I swerved to miss him and sideswiped the rear. I saw him go off of the road and I panicked. You have to believe me. I never meant for this to happen."

Krystal continued to pace, taking her time to stomach his pathetic excuse for allowing Antonio to remain in the ditch. Even if it was an accident, there was no excuse for him leaving the scene.

"Anything else you want to say before you meet your maker?"

"Only one thing." Octavio closed his eyes and sank into the comfort of the bed. He was sure this was the end. In a strange way, he was okay with that. "I love you, Krystal. I didn't think it was possible, but somehow I've fallen in love with you." He opened his eyes to the barrel of the pistol aimed just above the bridge of his nose.

"Good-bye, Octavio. I hope you find peace on the other side."

The weapon weighed down her arm. It felt heavier than it had even moments before. She stared into his eyes, burning his face into her subconscious. His image joined the others, her friends and family that were lost. In her mind, she lit a fire beneath it, watching as the image photograph singed and melted until only a mass of ash remained.

Something inside of Krystal snapped when she pulled the trigger. If she didn't know any better, she'd have sworn she heard the sound of something inside of her shattering into a million pieces. She heard voices all around her, the voices of friends she'd had to say good-bye to over the years. Antonio's voice popped in and out of her head on a whim, but it was Jerad's voice that stuck in her mind. It was Jerad's voice telling her she'd fulfilled her destiny and now it was time to go home.

The deed now done, she slid the gun into her bag along with the used wineglasses. She poured the remainder of the bottle's content down the drain and packed away the bottle, the file containing all of the information about her and Yohan, as well as the vial of ketamine she'd used to drug Octavio. And as she closed the front door, a sense of vindication washed over her. It was over. All of it was finally over.

Chapter Thirty-one

Yohan flipped open his ringing cell phone. He didn't bother to look at the caller ID. He assumed it was either Aubrey or Andre checking in. They'd all been riding around the city for hours trying to locate Krystal. He was hoping one of them had found her because he was starting to worry.

"Talk to me," Yohan said, not giving the individual on the other end the opportunity to greet him.

"Come get me."

Yohan slammed on his brakes at the sound of Krystal's voice. He ignored the screeching tires and honking horns surrounding him on all sides. He didn't even take a moment to make sure he hadn't caused an accident.

"Where are you?"

"Umm . . ." Krystal scanned the area for an identifiable landmark. "I'm in the Laundromat by the Kroger's on Tara Boulevard."

"Stay there. I'm about fifteen minutes away."

As he pulled back into traffic, he dialed Aubrey's cell.

"Yeah," Aubrey answered.

"Found her."

"Where is she?"

"Somewhere off of Tara Boulevard. I'm on my way to get her now. We'll meet you back at my place."

"I'll call Dre and let him know."

Ten minutes later, Yohan pulled into a parking spot in front of the place Krystal talked about. He watched her hand a little Hispanic girl a quarter for the gumball machine as he cut off the engine. Taking a deep breath, he climbed from the truck and made his way to the entrance of the establishment.

She turned in his direction as the door opened. She just stared at him with empty eyes. She stood and made her way over to him, her makeup caked on and her cheeks streaked where her mascara had run. She collapsed in his arms, too drained to support her weight, the burdens in her heart so heavy she no longer cared.

Yohan scooped her into his arms, carrying her to the truck. When she was settled in, he climbed into the driver's seat, not knowing what to say to her. Gripping the steering wheel, trying his best to control his anger, Yohan counted to ten before he spoke. "Talk to me, Krystal."

"I need to go home." She couldn't hide the tremble in her voice. She was hurting and she was on the verge of giving up on everything.

"I just want to make sure you're not hurt, then we can go."

"You don't understand! I need to go home, Yohan! I need to go home." Krystal only wanted one thing right now and that was her mother. She'd been away from home far too long. After what she'd just done, all she wanted to do was crawl into her mother's arms and cry.

Yohan looked over at her, finally understanding what she meant by *home*. He started the truck and pulled out of the parking lot. He wasn't sure how he felt about her sudden need to go to the place that had driven her into his life. He agreed that sooner or later she needed to mend things with her family. He thought it a shame they'd missed out on so much. Still, not knowing why she'd had such a sudden change of heart bothered him.

Parking in his usual spot, Yohan killed the engine. He turned to face her, not sure how she'd react to him speaking. She'd been silent the majority of the trip, only answering yes when he asked again if she was all right.

"You know, they're upstairs waiting for us," he finally said.

Krystal looked up at the lights on in their apartment. "I guess they're pissed, huh?"

"I don't think any of us are mad at you. We've all just been worried sick. We've been driving around the city for hours looking for you."

"I'm sorry." She lowered her head. "I didn't mean to have y'all worried."

"Krystal." He narrowed his eyes before continuing. "What happened tonight?"

She turned from him, not wanting to tell him the gruesome deed she'd performed. But she had to tell him. She had to tell them all. "Let's go upstairs; I want to get this over with."

Swinging the door open with a newfound confidence, she stepped from the vehicle. She was tired—tired of being without her parents, tired of pretending everything was just fine, tired of everything—and she just needed to rest. She flung open the apartment door.

"Where the hell have you been?" Aubrey yelled.

She didn't acknowledge the question. Instead, she walked right past him. Stopping at the kitchen table, she slammed down the .45 she'd used to do the deed. "It's got a body tied to it. Y'all might want to get rid of it."

Then she turned and slammed the bedroom door closed behind her.

"What is she talking about?" Aubrey asked Yohan.

"I haven't the slightest idea."

"Did she say anything?"

"No, just that she wanted to go home."

"Home? Home as in . . ." Aubrey wanted to make sure he understood.

"I think Krystal needs her parents."

"We need to find out what happened tonight."

"I'll go talk to her." Yohan disappeared through the door to the bedroom, leaving Aubrey and Dre standing in the living room perplexed.

"What do you think happened?" Andre asked.

"I haven't the slightest. I don't even know where she got the gun from. It's not one of ours." Aubrey ran his hand through his hair. His head was beginning to hurt.

"What about her going home?"

"If that's what she wants, we don't have much of a choice. I'll make some kind of arrangements with the school once we figure out how long she's going to be gone."

"It's not fair." Andre slammed his fist against the table. "She's already been through so much."

Dre's attention turned toward the darkened hallway. He wished he could just make this go away. Krystal was so young to have seen and experienced all that she'd been through. He just wished there was some way for him to take away her pain. All he wanted for her was happiness. But if she'd done any of the things racing through his mind, he didn't know if she'd ever truly know happiness again.

"Krystal?" Yohan watched as she walked back and forth from the closet, stuffing clothes into a duffel bag.

She didn't look up at him; she just continued the pattern, back and forth, back and forth. He soon realized the actions were involuntary. She was running on autopilot, her mind trapped in some memory she wasn't quite ready to face.

She turned to walk back to the closet and he caught her around the waist, stopping her in mid-step. She struggled, trying with all of her strength to get away, but failing. Finally, the rocking began and the tears soon followed.

"Krystal, baby, tell me what happened," he urged.

"I had to do it. He couldn't get away with it. I couldn't let him live knowing what he'd done. I had to do it. I had to do it," she repeated again and again and again.

"Krystal! Krystal, listen to me. Calm down. Did someone try to hurt you?" he asked, trying to get information out of her one piece at a time.

"No."

"Did someone try to hurt one of your friends?"

"He killed him, Yohan. He thought it was you but he killed him. He killed Antonio and he wanted to kill you and I just couldn't let that happen. You always said we take care of our own, that no matter what you protect family. I did it to protect you. I did it to protect us." The words poured from her mouth one by one. Her mind didn't process the thoughts; her mouth just expelled everything racing through her mind.

"Who, Krystal? Who killed Antonio?" Yohan had his hands wrapped around her wrists. He tightened his grip, trying to make sense of what she was telling him.

"Ouch. Yohan, stop. You're hurting me." She tried to twist out of his grasp but he hung on, his hands squeezing so much that her fingers began to tingle.

"Tell me, Krystal!" He started to shake her. "Tell me who killed Antonio."

"Yohan! Let me go! You're hurting me!" Somehow she managed to get one hand free. She dug her nails into his wrist and he ultimately let go of her other arm. She plopped down on the bed, rubbing each wrist where he'd held her too tightly.

"I'm sorry." Yohan backed away from her, sure if he touched her again he'd hurt her. He never meant to cause her any harm, but he needed to know who killed his best friend.

Eventually, Krystal reached into the bag she'd carried with her when she did the deed, and pulled out the file. She held it out for him, and making a conscious effort not to touch her hand, Yohan took the file from her grasp.

He read the pages and pages of handwritten notes and logs. He flipped through the pictures, some of him, some of his truck, and the few of Krystal. He didn't know how to feel, he didn't know how to act, he was at a total loss for what to think or do. All of this time and his past had finally caught up with him.

"I should have listened to him," Yohan whispered, not intending for Krystal to hear.

"What did you say?"

He looked up at her, realizing she'd heard what he'd said. "Antonio told me to keep a lookout for someone tailing me. A few days later I noticed this red truck following me." It started to sink in. That wasn't the first time he'd seen that red truck; he'd seen it a couple of times before at Krystal's school. And if he didn't know any better, he'd have sworn he saw it at the club as well.

"Octavio." She closed her eyes, lowered her head and shook it.

"How did you find out?" He didn't look at her. She knew too much and he wanted to know why.

Krystal stood and made her way to the sliding glass door. She slid the door open and stepped into the night.

She needed air, she needed space, and she needed to not have to answer that question. But she'd anticipated this, had thought through a number of embellishments and convinced herself she had the perfect story when the question came. And yet here she was, faced with the question and not sure what the answer should be.

"Krystal?"

She turned to see Yohan standing at the door. His expression clearly showed the concern in his heart. His question had so many possible answers and she was sure he was preparing himself for the worst.

"One last secret," she replied softly, not really answering his question but attempting to convince herself that it was best for her to tell him everything.

He stepped a little closer, lessening the distance but leaving more than an arm's length between them. "What secret?"

Krystal gathered her thoughts, deciding it would be best if she told Yohan everything. "Do you remember a few weeks ago when you came to get me from school and you asked me who was the guy I was talking to?"

"Yeah."

"Well, that was Octavio. I met him the day I went to the park when I was suspended from school. Long story short, I guess he decided to use me to get to you."

"So you've been cheating on me?" Yohan was proud of hiding his emotions. Now was not the time for anger. He'd deal with that later.

"No. It wasn't like that."

"Then what was it like?" His voice rose just a tad. *So much for keeping the temper under control.*

"Sometimes I just needed someone to talk to, and sometimes you weren't around."

"So you ran to another man."

"He was just a friend." *Or so I thought.* "Besides, we only went out once."

"When?" Yohan's voice calmed. He needed know the truth.

"That night at Triple Threat."

"You came to the club with him?"

"I caught the bus to the club. He just met me there."

"I can't believe this!" What little control he'd regained rushed from his body. His hands balled into fists. Yohan stopped his initial reaction, focusing his attention on keeping his hands from reaching out to grab her.

"I'm sorry, Yohan. It never dawned on me that he might just be using me to get to you. But after Antonio died, I started to put things together. And when Aubrey told me about the red paint, I knew. The night I went to confront him, I discovered the file and the white paint on his truck."

"Why didn't you come to me then? I could have taken care of this."

"No! When I figured out he was the one who'd killed Antonio, it was personal. And then to find out he was using me to get to you. I couldn't just walk away." She hoped he understood. Prayed that he would.

"So you took matters into your own hands."

"I did what I had to do." There would be no more tears. She allowed the anger to consume her. She narrowed her eyes at him. She refused to let him make her feel guilty for handling business.

Yohan didn't know what to think. He just stared at her, trying to figure all of this out. "Who gave you the gun?"

"Can't tell you that. I promised to keep the person I got it from out of this."

"Fine. I'll let you take that up with Brey and Dre. Where's the body?"

"In his hotel room. The room key and his car keys are in my bag." She walked back into the bedroom. Rambling through the bag, she handed him the keys, a piece of stationery with the address and the room number on it, the remainder of the clear liquid she'd used to drug him, and the glass Octavio drank from.

"What's the glass for?"

"I drugged him with the stuff in the vial."

"Are you sure no one saw you?"

"Positive. I kept gloves on the entire time and I have the glass that I drank from. I made sure not to leave anything behind."

"One last thing." Yohan took in a deep breath. He wasn't sure he really wanted to know the answer to the question in his mind. But deep down he needed to know.

"What?"

"Did anything ever happen between you two?"

"No." Her answer came across very clear. "Nothing. Not even a peck on the cheek."

Releasing a breath, Yohan turned from her and headed toward the door. He needed to let Brey and Dre know what happened.

"Hey." Krystal stopped him as he turned to walk through the door.

"What?" He hadn't meant for the word to come out short, but he'd said it now.

"Why was he after you?" The *why* was the only missing piece of information she failed to get from Octavio before she killed him. She understood that Yohan's past was something he didn't talk about. But Antonio had died because of it, and she wanted an answer.

"Before I came here, I hooked up with this girl and let's just say her parents weren't exactly fond of me. She died in a car accident on her way home from my spot, and of course, they blamed me. Her death was ruled an accident, but her parents wouldn't let up so I skipped town. I guess they sent him to try to find me." Yohan abruptly turned and walked out the door, closing it shut behind him. He didn't want to explain any more. Losing Miranda had been hard, but he'd gotten over it and he didn't want to talk about it ever again.

"So?" Aubrey asked, watching Yohan rounding the corner from the bedrooms.

"I have an address and keys." He waved the piece of paper and jingled the keys.

"What did she say?"

"The guy killed Antonio." He relinquished the stuff to Aubrey.

"What the—"

Yohan cut Andre off before his temper took over. "Look, when he hit the truck, he thought I was driving. I'll explain later. We don't have time for this. The body's still in his hotel room and we need to figure out how to get rid of it."

"Already taken care of." Aubrey picked up his cell phone and made a brief call. "Stay here with Krystal. We'll take care of everything else."

As they turned to leave, Yohan stopped them. "What about her going home?"

"She's grown; if she wants to go home, take her home." Aubrey turned and followed his brother out of the door. They had a mess to clean up, and they just hoped no one saw or heard what Krystal had done.

Chapter Thirty-two

Aubrey rubbed the bridge of his nose, attempting to will away the headache he'd been contending with for hours. His head shook as he tried to make sense of the entire situation. His mind refused to comprehend the truth: Krystal had killed a man.

"I guess she's one of us now," the man sitting to Aubrey's right finally said.

Aubrey turned to face Raffaele, the eldest, most respected member of their extended family. Before commenting, he glanced at the other two men hovering in opposite corners of the room.

"No. I don't want her pulled into this," Aubrey replied.

"Surely you believe she's earned the protection of this family. I mean, she did avenge the death of one of our own."

"I'm not saying she doesn't deserve the protection. But she's had it since she got here. She was to be protected because of Jerad."

"A compromise, then?" Raffaele asked, perching his fingertips into a tent of flesh at chest level.

"What kinda compromise?"

"She continues to receive the shadowed protection from the family. We'll make sure no one finds out what she's done and we'll keep her as far away from the other aspects of the family business as possible. However, you do realize she'll always be a potential target should anyone choose to come after us."

"I know. I'll eventually tell her everything. But until then, I'm putting her safety in Yohan's and the family's hands."

"Agreed. You still haven't told us how she was able to find out who'd killed Antonio."

"Apparently, my brother was killed in a case of mistaken identity. From what I've gathered from Yohan, the guy Krystal killed was using her to get to him. When he ran the truck off of the road, he thought it was Yohan."

"And why exactly was this man after Yohannes?"

"That only Yohan and Antonio know. Antonio took the secret to the grave and Yohan's not saying a word. I also suspect Krystal knows, but she too is keeping tight lips."

"Sounds to me like Mr. Hampton may be more of a liability than we need, especially if the fate of our new sister lies in his hands." Raffaele twirled the diamond ring on his finger, paying more attention to it than to Aubrey.

"With all due respect, I disagree. I still think Yohan is more of an asset than a liability."

"And how exactly is that?" Raffaele pulled the handkerchief from his suit pocket and proceeded to wipe off the diamond-studded ring. He waited patiently, not turning his eyes in the direction of Aubrey.

"Since she came here, Krystal has been Yohan's primary responsibility. This act of revenge was Krystal's idea. I'm pretty sure that if she'd confided in him, he'd have done the same thing, not just to protect himself but to protect his family. Krystal means the world to him and outside of us, he's all she has left right now."

"Your point would be?" Raffaele asked, growing impatient with Aubrey's partial explanation.

"My point is, what happened with Krystal was a fluke. I've seen what Yohan is capable of when it come to Krystal, and who better to protect her than someone who is already as close to her as he is."

"And how does the younger Fedichi feel about all of this?"

"He agrees that Yohan is the best protection for Krystal."

"You don't believe his personal feelings toward her will ever cloud his judgment should the time arise when he must make a life-or-death decision?" Leaning back into the chair, the man replaced the handkerchief.

"Yohan will do anything in his power to insure Krystal is never put in a situation as such; but if by chance she ends up in some life-or-death situation, I am more than confident Yohan would give his own life for hers."

"Then unless anyone has anything else to add,"—Raffaele carefully observe his comrades before continuing— "I believe that you have made an informed decision regarding the future care of our new sister. We will remain in the shadows contingent upon Yohannes's continual fulfillment of his duties as Krystal's primary guardian. Should she ever need us, though, we will insure her continued safety."

"My brother and I thank you."

"And where exactly is the younger Fedichi?" Raffaele expected to see both at this meeting. When Aubrey showed up alone, he was more than a little disturbed.

"He's with the others cleaning up Krystal's mess. He said something about wanting to see the face of the man who took Tonio away."

Chapter Thirty-three

Home. Seemed like only yesterday home was a distant memory to be cherished, controlled, even locked away when the need to return arose. Now, within twenty minutes, Krystal would set foot in a world she hadn't been a part of in far too long.

"Can we make a stop?" she asked as Yohan pulled off of the expressway.

"Where?" He rolled to a halt in the gas station to fill the tank. They still had a little further to go, and they both needed to stretch their legs.

"I need to say good-bye to him."

He understood Krystal now. He'd seen her contend with Jerad's death and he knew when they came here she'd want to finally visit the grave. He could tell Krystal was truly ready for closure. She wanted to get on with her life, and in order to do that, she needed to pay her last respects to the only other man she'd ever truly loved.

He didn't respond to her immediately. Instead, he worked through his feelings as the gas pumped into the truck. He considered what her final good-bye meant for them. In the last few weeks, their world had been thrust into utter chaos. And the wild ride was still not over. Besides visiting the grave of her long-lost love, Krystal was just about to show up on her parents' doorstep. They'd had no contact for nearly five years, save for the few messages sent through her sister. They knew she was alive, they probably even knew she was well, but they had no idea what she'd been through and no idea she was about to reenter their lives.

Sliding back into the driver's seat, Yohan turned to her. "Where to?"

He followed her directions down Pontchartrain Boulevard to the Metairie Cemetery. Though she'd never been able to make it to his grave, Krystal knew the exact spot where Jerad's body lay. Yohan put the borrowed truck in park and turned off the engine. The only sound that could be heard was that of the fan cooling the engine.

He looked around at the aboveground tombs and marble statues of saints and angels. He'd never seen anything like this. Many of the monuments to the dead appeared to be in perfect condition though he knew they were centuries old.

Krystal remained absorbed with her own thoughts, staring out of the window.

"You sure you're up to this?" He watched a lone tear slide down her cheek, wondering if she was strong enough to do this right now.

"I have to do this. It's the only way I'll finally be able to get on with my life."

He intertwined his fingers with hers, not knowing what else to do. He agreed she needed to do this, but her tears were far from reassuring.

"You don't have to do this now. If you're not ready, Krystal, then give yourself some time."

"No. I have to do this now. I can't go back to my parents' house with this hung over my head. I've already got enough to explain. I just need to see him one last time. Ya know, speak my piece."

"You know where the grave is?"

"Yeah." She turned from him to stare out of the passenger side window. "It's the dark gray marble stone just below the angel."

"Do you want me to come with you?"

"No. I need to do this on my own." With her free hand Krystal reached for the door, but before she could push the button to unlock it, Yohan turned her to face him.

"Listen, Krystal, if you need me for anything, I'm here. You aren't alone in any of this. We've decided to stand by each other no matter what, and that means you allowing me to help you and vice versa. I know you're independent and I wouldn't want you any other way. I know you're strong and that's one of the many wonderful things I love about you. But baby, I know when it comes to Jerad, you still harbor a lot of anger, hurt, and resentment. This isn't just an ending for you; it's a beginning for us, and I want to be by your side."

He watched the involuntary quiver of her bottom lip. He wanted so much to reach over, draw her into his arms, and kiss her. He fought the urge, though. Passion was the last thing she needed right now.

They walked hand in hand, side by side, in silence. The air carried the stillness of death here. No breeze, no birds, no sign of life other than the fullness of the grass and the two bodies approaching the gray stone marker of the deceased.

A few steps before reaching the grave, Krystal stopped. Her sudden movement tugged on his hand.

"What's wrong?"

"I want to go the rest of the way alone."

"Krystal . . ."

"Please," she interrupted. "I have to do this on my own. I have to face this just like I found him."

She started her path to her new beginning alone. With each step, the images of what she'd shared with Jerad burst to life in her mind. By the time she reached the place where her first love would rest for all eternity, tears streamed from her eyes. She collapsed the moment she read the words, *live life love life*, above his name carved in the stone.

Immediately Yohan appeared at her side, trying his best to help her from the ground. But Krystal fought him, just like she'd fought him the night she told them about how she'd found Jerad. She needed to let it all pour out of her. Tearing away at the wall she'd erected around any part of her being that still held on to Jerad, Krystal cried and screamed and cursed and relived everything for the last time. She understood that she'd always remember him, but after she'd let it all out, she was confident she'd be able to get on with her life.

With the cleansing of her heart, mind, and soul complete, she laid her palm against the cool marble. She spoke a short prayer of love, adoration, and forgiveness to her lost love. Then she gathered her thoughts and reached out to her future.

Yohan helped her from the ground, pulling her securely into his arms and comforting her as best he could. She trembled against his chest, trying to control the emotions pouring from her soul. After a few minutes of her crying, she calmed enough to speak.

"Thank you," she said to him.

He just smiled down at her, not saying a word. He scooped her up in his arms and carried her back to the truck. She needed to rest. Her day was far from over and she'd need every ounce of strength left when she returned to her parents' home.

* * *

Yohan and Krystal sat in her parents' driveway for half an hour before she finally built up enough nerve to go to the door. The house remained just as she remembered it. The outside appeared to have been freshly painted a light beige and the sand-colored brick showed signs of a fresh pressure washing. Her mother's roses flourished as the vines weaved in and out of the white wooden trellises on either side of the stairs leading up to the front door.

They saw no indication of anyone in the house, but Krystal knew they were there. Her parents retired a year or so before she'd left, and unless they were out shopping, one or both of them should be home. From the corner of her eye, she watched Yohan watching her.

"What?" she asked, tired of him staring at her.

"I didn't say anything."

"Maybe not, but that look you're giving me says it all."

"I'm just waiting for you to decide what you want to do. This is your call."

"You know, I never thought I'd see this place again." She lowered her head as shame washed over her.

"Why?"

"I don't know. I just figured this was my past. This place held some good times. I've just spent so much time remembering the bad times that they overshadowed what should have been most important. Like that tree over there." She pointed to a large tree hung with Spanish moss. The upper leaves and branches were visible from the street, but the privacy fence hid the trunk. "Some nights I'd meet Jerad under the tree and we'd talk till dawn. A tire used to hang from it and me and Myisha would swing for hours on it after school. I miss that, you know. I just wanted things to always be that way."

"As children we all do. Sooner or later we grow up

and wish for those things back." He covered her hand with his. "Some of them we can get back, some of them we can't. Can I ask you something?"

"I guess."

"Is that why you spend so much time in the park at home? It reminds you of your time with Jerad."

Krystal considered his question before responding. She'd never really thought about why she spent so much time in the park in Lincoln Heights; she just knew that a sense of calm surrounded her whenever she was there.

"Now that you mention it, you could be right."

"Look, I know I can never replace Jerad. Likewise, you know I'd never want to. What you two shared was no doubt special. I want what we have to remain special in its own way. I don't ever want you to think the little things don't matter to me because they do. Each moment I spend with you creates a new, wonderful memory that I will cherish for years to come. I just hope one day you'll think the same of your time spent with me."

"I already do." She leaned over and kissed the man she was learning to love all over again. Taking a deep breath, she said to him, "I'm ready to go in."

"Just remember, no matter what, I love you."

"I love you too."

Exiting the vehicle and walking around to the passenger side, Yohan helped Krystal from the truck. They stood side by side at the door as she rang the doorbell. She inched her way behind him as she heard the lock turn.

When the door swung open, Yohan had to look down to see the tiny woman in linen pants and a floral blouse. She appeared to be in her mid- to late-forties with streaks of silver scattered throughout her jet black hair. He smiled as he realized Krystal was a much younger version of her mother.

"Can I help you, young man?"

Yohan looked to his left, sure Krystal was still standing beside him, only to find her gone. Turning his head a little further, he caught a glimpse of her burgundy hair blowing in the breeze. He was much taller and significantly larger than Krystal, so it was easy for her to hide behind him. He reached his hand back for her and immediately she intertwined her fingers with his.

"Are you Ms. Bao?"

"Yes," she replied.

"You may want to get your husband."

"Whatever for?" The woman's nervousness manifested itself by a light shuffling of her feet.

"Trust me, he should be by your side."

Yohan rubbed Krystal's hand with his thumb as he waited for Mr. Bao to join his wife at the front door.

Krystal's father was a man of stature just like Yohan. Looking at him, Yohan understood Krystal's love of larger men. The man standing before him was only a few inches shorter but similar in build. His cotton shirt fit loosely around his healthy physique, while his slacks rested tightly around the muscles in his legs.

"Can we help you?" he finally asked Yohan. He didn't like the fact that this stranger was scaring his wife.

"There's someone here to see you."

The couple looked at each other, still not understanding why this man was at their door. Yohan stepped to the side, allowing them to get their first look at a daughter they hadn't seen in nearly five years.

"Hi Mom, Dad."

Krystal's mother swayed. Her father caught her before her legs completely gave way. Scooping her into his arms, he carried her to the couch, beckoning Krystal and Yohan in. So much needed to be said, and tonight everything would be out in the open.

Epilogue

After taking six months after her high school graduation to mend things with her parents, Krystal dove into her first semester at Georgia State University. She stayed on campus her first two years and for the first time, Yohan realized how empty his home was without her. With the blessing of Aubrey, Andre, and her parents, Yohan proposed to Krystal on the anniversary of the day The Trio had brought her to Lincoln Heights.

He remembered how her eyes had glazed over while she stared at the ring in his hand. As the first tears crawled down her cheeks, she'd made him the happiest man on earth. They'd been married for two years now, and their first child was due in five days.

"Krystal Bao-Hampton," the announcer called.

Yohan beamed with pride as his nine-month pregnant wife waddled her way across the stage. She'd worked herself nearly to death making sure she completed all of her assignments and tests weeks in advance, just in case the baby decided to make an unexpected early appearance.

He was so proud of her.

Krystal rubbed her belly as she walked across the gym floor. The baby had been kicking her since early this morning. Strangely, the kicks were higher than usual and more frequent than she'd ever experienced.

She gave a weak smile at her husband, family, and friends as she followed the procession back to her seat. Once comfortable, she rocked back and forth, trying to soothe her baby. When the last name was called, Krystal released a sigh of relief. She'd worked hard for this and she was glad she was able to make it through the ceremony.

Following her fellow graduates into the courtyard, she took a seat on a vacant bench to wait for Yohan and the others to join her. The sky was clear and a light breeze cooled her skin from the warmth of the sun. A smile crept across her lips as she watched her hubby approach.

"You okay?" he asked, wrapping her in his arms and pulling her close.

"Yeah, your son is just having himself a swimming good time."

"I think your daughter is trying to tell you it's time to get home to a hot bath and some relaxation."

He and Krystal joked constantly about the sex of the baby. They'd chosen to wait until it was born to find out if they had a son or a daughter. It really didn't matter to either of them. As long as the child was healthy, they'd make sure he or she was happy.

"Congratulations, baby. We're proud of you," Ms. Bao exclaimed as she joined the small crowd of people surrounding Krystal.

"Thanks, Mom. I'm glad y'all could make it. You coming to the house?"

"We wouldn't miss it for the world."

Yohan had planned a small get-together for Krystal at the apartment. It would be their last there. He closed on their house in two days, and they hoped to be moved in before the baby came.

Yohan helped Krystal from the bench. After everyone hugged her, they turned to walk to the parking lot. The sound of someone calling her name stopped her. She froze when she looked into the face she hadn't seen in many years.

"Jerad would have been proud," the man said to her as he captured her in a warm embrace.

"It's so good to see you."

"It's good to see you too. Now let me get a good look at you."

Krystal stepped back far enough for Jerad's father to get a good look at her and her swollen belly. He looked her over one good time. He hadn't seen her since Antonio's funeral. He'd wanted to talk to her then, but she was so distraught he didn't want to cause her any additional pain by bringing up Jerad.

"So when's the baby due?"

"Next week." Again she rubbed her stomach. She felt her unborn child swimming around and the extra movement was a little disconcerting.

"Cutting it kinda close, aren't you?"

"Actually, I'm ready. It could come today as far as I'm concerned."

"Well, I'm not going to keep you. I just came to tell you congratulations and to give you something I know Jerad wanted you to have." He reached into his pocket and pulled out two velvet boxes. He handed the first box to her, watching intensely as she opened the lid.

Krystal reached for the chain around her neck as she stared into the box.

"I guess he really did leave you his heart." Jerad's father pulled the other half of the locket from the confines of the box and snapped it onto the half hanging from Krystal's neck.

She felt the burning behind her eyes but fought back the tears. "Thank you," she managed, trying her best to control the quiver in her voice.

"There's one other thing. Whether or not he thought you should have it, I think you should." He handed her the second box, giving her the time to take in the sight as she opened it.

"I can't take this," she said, shaking her head from side to side.

"Yes, you can. It's at Aubrey's house waiting for you. You know, I think the only thing he loved in this world more than that car was you."

"I don't know what to say."

"Just say that you'll take care of it as well as you took care of my son the last years of his life."

"I will. I promise."

They hugged again, sharing a moment no one else could understand. When Krystal pulled away, her cheeks were kissed with fresh tears. Just then, she doubled over as her unborn child delivered a fierce kick. Then she felt it—the warm moisture flowing from her body.

"Are you all right?"

"Yeah." Krystal turned to face the crowd of her family and friends. They'd busied themselves catching up, giving her some time alone to talk with Jerad's father.

"Ah, Yohan, honey."

Yohan turned in her direction, seeing the concern in her face. He rushed to her side, wanting to make sure she was okay.

"I think my warm bath and relaxation are going to have to wait."

"What's wrong?"

"Our delivery is coming a little sooner than anticipated. My water just broke."

"Come on. Let's get you to the hospital."

As Yohan helped Krystal into the elevator, Jerad's father informed everyone that Krystal was going into labor. They all appeared to be really excited. He turned to walk away when Aubrey stopped him.

"I know this is hard for you, but you're still family and I think Jerad would have wanted you to be here for Krystal." Aubrey hoped he'd stay. He understood what this day meant, but Krystal needed him there as much as she needed everyone else.

"What about her parents? Do they know who I am?"

"They know. We're all family now, and I think they are finally beginning to understand the bond Krystal and Jerad shared. They've been out of her life almost as long as you have. Everything's out in the open. It's been a struggle, but they've come a long way."

Jerad's father spent most of Krystal's labor filtering questions from her parents. They'd totally misunderstood his son's intentions toward their daughter. He told them of the heart-to-heart talks he'd had with Jerad regarding Krystal. He informed them of Jerad's decision to marry her when she turned eighteen. Jerad wanted so much for her, but he never dealt with the grief of losing his mother so he decided to take his own life to be with her.

Krystal's mother found the information troublesome. All of these years they'd denied her the opportunity to be with Jerad, thinking he was taking advantage of her. Now that they knew the truth, Ms. Bao wasn't sure how she felt.

Krystal had lost the one person who'd meant the world to her, and they hadn't even allowed her to go to the funeral and say her final good-byes. Her heart ached for her daughter. She decided then, that no matter what, she'd find a way to make this up to her. They'd been hard on her, but Krystal proved she was strong. Ms. Bao no longer blamed her daughter for leaving them. She now blamed herself.

Yohan entered the waiting area where Aubrey, Andre, Krystal's parents, her sister, and Jerad's father had spent the past few hours. All eyes turned to him, anxiously awaiting any news on Krystal and the baby. He smiled at them all, reassuring them that everything was just as it should be.

"Everyone ready to meet the new addition to our ever-growing family?"

They each spoke or nodded their confirmation as they followed Yohan down the hallway to Krystal's private room. One by one they took peeks at the bundle of joy Krystal held in her arms. Only Jerad's father lingered in the background.

"Mr. Anderson," Krystal finally spoke to the figure hovering in the corner like a frightened child. Jerad's father looked up at her smiling face. "Did you look at the baby's name?"

He looked down at the name card attached to the makeshift bassinet all hospitals provided for new mothers. Reading the name, he quickly looked back up in her direction.

"You didn't have to name him—"

"Yes,"—Krystal wrapped her free hand around Yohan's and looked up at him before continuing—"we did. Jerad delivered this child to us today and it's only fitting he be named after the two people who meant the world to us. Do you remember what time he was born?"

Mr. Anderson thought back to the day his son made his entrance into this world. "Two-oh-six P.M. Why?"

"Look at the time on the card."

Mr. Anderson couldn't believe it. Not only did Krystal's son share Jerad's birthday and name, but he was also born at the exact time Jerad had been born.

"Now do you understand why I say your son delivered Jerad Antonio Hampton into this world?"

He nodded his confirmation as Krystal beckoned him to come get a glimpse of the little boy the love of his son's life had brought into this world.